The Year of the Elm

Published by
Mark Barrett

Cover by
Joleene Naylor

The Year of the Elm
Copyright © 2010 by Mark Barrett
All rights reserved.

ISBN 978-1-7350520-2-1

*for Claire and Kellen
daughter and son*

CONTENTS

APPLE PIE

~ May ~

I hit the ball harder than I'd hit it all day and it went way over Bucky's head. He threw his glove up at it and missed, then walked after it real slow. The ball rolled to a stop by the goalpost, and when Bucky finally got to it he picked it up like it weighed ten pounds. "Throw it in!" I yelled.

"Forget it," Bucky said, and I knew he wasn't going to throw it in. He got his glove and tossed the ball up and caught it while he was walking back. Then he did it again and dropped it. I looked past him at how close I'd come to hitting the fence behind the goalpost.

For a minute I thought someday I'd hit that fence, and maybe even hit past it, but it was a long way, and the more I thought about it the more I thought maybe I never really would. I turned around and looked across the field at our school, and I saw how blue and clear the sky had gotten while we'd been playing. The breeze was warm and the sun was hot, and all of a sudden it felt like that first real summer day we get every year in Summit, where you know it's summer because you can feel it, and not because the calendar says so.

It seems like I notice it each year, like that day when you can feel winter coming right through your clothes, even if the sun is out and the trees still have leaves. Mom says she likes all the weather we get, like me, but Dad says there's only three good days a year in Iowa, and since one of them is in the middle of winter you better enjoy the other two.

Across the field some big kids were riding their bikes up and down the hill by the school. They looked big enough to be in junior high, and I thought maybe they played on one of the football teams that used the field. I watched them riding and crashing down the hill on purpose until Bucky came walking up, kicking the ball.

"You gonna play football?" I said.

"I don't know," he said. "Maybe. You?"

"Mom says I can't. Dad says maybe, but Mom's afraid I'll get my leg broken. Or my neck."

"Yeah," Bucky said. "Pete Bonner's big brother busted his collarbone in high school."

I looked at Bucky. "What's a collarbone?"

Bucky pulled his shirt down and pointed at two skinny bones, one on each side of his neck. "These here," he said. I felt mine and got kinda sick thinking about them being broken. "Busted right out through the skin too," he said.

"Shut up," I said, and quit touching my bones, but I could still feel them and they started to hurt.

"What do you want to do?" Bucky said.

I didn't know what I wanted to do. Usually we'd go over to Bucky's house for a drink of water after we played at the field, since it's a lot closer than my house.

But Bucky was spending the night so his mom could get a bunch of homework done for college, and when she dropped him off with his stuff she told us about ten times not to bother her for anything. Bucky's mom can be crabbier than any mom I know, so that was the last place I was gonna say we should go.

"Let's go home," I said. "Mom said she might get Popsicles at the store."

"Okay," Bucky said.

I kicked the head of the bat with my feet as we walked, and Bucky threw the ball into his glove so it would make a loud slap, but it almost never did. We cut through the school fence and went past the old-folk's home, and even during the day the big house was scary. A couple of times on my way home from Bucky's I had cut through when it was getting dark, and inside I could see funny lamps and shadows moving around. I walked by the place just about every day, going to school and coming home, and I could never get over the feeling that the old people inside were watching me. Sometimes, if I was alone, I'd get about halfway past and then just start running, even if I was trying not to.

When we got up to Summit Street we had to wait at the corner for a couple of cars to go by, so I looked up and down the block at all the big houses. Some of them were huge, and most of them had big old elms out front, the branches growing together over the street like a big leafy tunnel.

I looked at the biggest house, a brick one with big white pillars out front and a driveway that went back around the side. It was the house that sat up across the alley from ours, but it was twice as big. Sometimes Bucky and me climbed into my tree house and watched the old lady who lived there while she was working in her flower garden. She had tons of flowers, so we were pretty sure she never noticed the ones we picked for our moms.

We crossed the street and went halfway down the block, then turned in the alley, keeping an eye on the first hedge because a mean kid lived behind it and he was always picking on us. After that was a yard without a fence, then we came to Mrs. Gale's yard, where we used to stop on the way home to pick apples or sour cherries or mulberries from her trees, if anything was growing. A year ago she put up a chain fence for a dog one of her boys got, which was good because the dog was big and mean, but a couple of months after that he moved and took the dog with him. Now the fence didn't do anything except make it harder to get stuff out of her trees without getting caught. If we kicked that fence even a little it sounded like it rattled all the way around the yard and right up to her house.

Mrs. Gale didn't care much about us taking stuff, but she was plenty scared we'd fall out of a tree and get hurt. I told her once about a time I fell out of a tree and landed on my head and didn't even need stitches, but she didn't think that proved anything.

"Looks like there's gonna be a lot of cherries this year," I said, leaning quiet on the fence and looking at Mrs. Gale's cherry tree. The cherries weren't near ripe, but you could see a lot of them. I looked at the apple tree but there weren't any apples showing yet.

"There's a few mulberries," Bucky said.

I looked over and I could see some purple berries hidden in the leaves that I hadn't seen at first. "Yeah," I said. "You wanna get some?"

"We'll get caught," he said. "We always get caught, unless it's at night. And even then we almost got caught that one time."

I looked between Mrs. Gale's house and garage, and I could see her car wasn't in the driveway where she usually parked. "I think she's gone," I said.

"There's somebody in that window," Bucky said. He bent down and pulled at some weeds, then looked up at the sky like there was something to see. I looked at the house but I couldn't see anybody.

I figured Bucky was lying to get out of sneaking over the fence, and I was thinking of slugging him, but right then Mrs. Gale's daughter, Hillary, stepped in front of the kitchen window. She was looking down at something, then I saw she was filling a glass in the sink. When it was full she picked up something on the counter that I couldn't see, ate it, took a drink, then looked out the window right at me. I kicked some gravel and pretended I was just standing there. "It's Hillary," I said.

Hillary used to babysit me and my sister Megan, but she hadn't done it lately because of all the things she was doing in high school. I wished she would quit all that stuff 'cause she was the best babysitter we ever had. She never made us go to bed on time and we almost always got popcorn or a treat, even if we didn't listen to her when she told us to do something.

I didn't think Hillary'd care if we were up in her mom's trees, but I wasn't sure so I decided to keep kicking gravel until she quit looking out the window. I tried watching her out the sides of my eyes, but that hurt and I couldn't see her anyway. Pretty quick Bucky said, "She still there?"

I lifted my head way up like I was looking at the sky, but really I was looking at the kitchen window. I could see Hillary still standing there, eating something, taking a drink, then eating something again. "Yeah," I said.

"Let's forget it," Bucky said. "I'd rather have Popsicles anyway." He turned and walked toward my house, kicking a rock in front of him.

"Wait," I said. I looked at the kitchen window again, then at the other windows at the back of the house, and I couldn't see Hillary anymore. "Come on," I said, running past Bucky and around the corner of the fence, into my yard.

I followed the fence past the big elm in the middle of the backyard, so tall its branches went from way up over the back of the house to all the way out by the alley. When the fence ran into the back of Mrs. Gale's garage I stopped, put down the bat, then started climbing over real quiet. It's best to climb there 'cause you can lean on the garage and it hides you from the house until you're all the way over.

"Wait!" Bucky said, running up behind me.

I stopped, hanging on the fence. "What?"

"What if we get caught?"

"So? Hillary ain't gonna call the cops or anything."

"What if she tells her mom, and her mom calls my mom?"

That made me think a minute, and the more I

thought about it the more I thought that would be worse than the police. But I could see the mulberries better from up on the fence, and they looked big and purple and really sweet. "Mrs. Gale doesn't know your mom," I said, thinking I wouldn't get in trouble even if Bucky's mom did get called. "And if she asks who your mom is, just say you don't know."

I climbed over quick and jumped down on the other side before Bucky could say anything. Bucky looked at me like he might run off. "Come on," I said. "Nothin's gonna happen."

Bucky looked around, then dropped his glove and ball and climbed up, and almost right away got his pants caught on the wire at the top of the fence. He tried to climb down the other side but almost fell over, then I had to hold him up while he got his pants unhooked. Even then he still fell on his butt.

"Stupid fence," he said, brushing his pants off.

We ran over to the mulberry tree but about halfway there Buck stepped in some old dog poo and said, "Yuck," way too loud. I gave him a dirty look but he didn't see it 'cause he was wiping his shoe off on the grass. He worked at it so hard the bottom of his shoe turned green and he wore a rut in Mrs. Gale's yard.

"Come on," I whispered, thinking I could feel Hillary staring at us from all of the windows at once. All of a sudden Bucky took off running like he just remembered where he was, and he woulda beat me to the tree but I held on to the back of his shirt so it was a tie.

We climbed into the tree real quick and it seemed a lot safer under all those drooping branches and leaves. I could see most of Mrs. Gale's house if I moved around, but I thought somebody would have to look pretty hard to spot us from any of the windows.

I climbed up a bit where I didn't have to reach out too far, and Buck stayed down low and walked out on a branch, holding on to another one over his head for balance. Up close I could see that most of the mulberries weren't ripe at all, and the ones that had started to turn purple were still hard when I squeezed them. I looked down at the branches below and I couldn't see any bird droppings, and on the ground there wasn't a single ripe berry where I knew there would be a mess in a few weeks.

"These aren't any good," Buck said, climbing across the tree to the other side.

"Yeah," I said. "The birds aren't even eating them."

Bucky kept trying berries and spitting them out. I put the purplest berry I could find in my mouth to see if I could suck some sweetness out of it, then I leaned back against the trunk and thought about all the things we were gonna do over the summer.

"Hey, Buck," I said.

"What?"

"Do we have to go to school Thursday, or is the last day Wednesday?"

"Thursday. We had those two snow days so we gotta make up a day."

"Oh, yeah," I said, thinking that was a cheat. It had been so cold both days we didn't get to go sledding or have any fun, which is what a snow day's supposed to be for. "So how come we only gotta make up one day?"

Buck spit out another berry and said, "They figure we're gonna miss at least one day anyway, so they plan for it in the schedule."

Right while he was talking Mrs. Gale walked under the tree with a bag of groceries and yelled, "What are you doing?!" It was so loud Bucky fell right out of the tree. One second he was standing on the branch, then the next he was standing on the ground by Mrs. Gale, looking like he didn't have any idea how he got there.

She looked down at Bucky, then up at me. Her face was all red and she was shaking like she was going to start yelling even louder. "Get down out of there right now," she said, grabbing her bag with both hands like it might fall out of her arms.

I swallowed the berry in my mouth, which was hard to do all of a sudden, and started climbing down. "Be careful!" she yelled, and it scared me so much I almost fell too. She must have said it fifty more times before I got down beside Bucky, who was shaking more than me and Mrs. Gale put together.

"Can't I go to the store for ten minutes without coming home and finding you boys up in my trees?" I got mad at myself for not remembering to be quiet, then I forgot about that and got kind of nervous be-cause Mrs. Gale looked real upset. Her eyes were kinda bugged out and watery, and lines were popping out on her forehead, and it gave me the creeps 'cause it looked like the man down the block that got the cops called on him one night for fighting with his wife. "Answer me!" she said.

"Don't call my mom!" Bucky said. "I won't ever do it again, I promise!"

Mrs. Gale looked at him and back at me. "What am I going to do? I can't have you climbing my trees. You could fall and get hurt! Very badly hurt!" She hugged the bag tighter and crumpled the top closed. "I can't have it anymore, do you understand me? It's got to stop."

I got a sick feeling and I thought about running, but I kept standing there with Mrs. Gale staring at me like she was waiting for an answer. "Just go home," she said. "Go home and don't come back or I'll have to call your parents." She looked right at Buck then and I knew I wouldn't get him back over the fence for a long time. "Go on," she said, pointing to the open gate by her driveway, and I could see her car was there now, parked where she always parked.

We ran to the gate and Bucky ran through and over to my house without looking back. I turned to latch the gate, mostly to keep Mrs. Gale from coming after us, but she was walking up to her back door. She grabbed the crumpled top of the bag in one hand and the door with the other, and right then the whole side of the bag ripped out. A bag of flour fell out and landed on the step with a big white puff, then a bunch of big green apples fell out and bounced down the stairs, rolling all over the place. Mrs. Gale grabbed the rest of the bag and held it against her but a little glass bottle slipped through her fingers and broke on the steps. Something that looked like runny syrup ran down onto the cement.

Mrs. Gale looked at the stuff on the ground and

started crying. She set the bag down and picked up a couple of the apples and cried harder, then just stood there with apples in her hands, crying into the back of her arm. It made me scared because she was crying like my mom cried after she smashed my sister's finger.

I didn't think I should keep standing there so I left and went across Mrs. Gale's driveway and our driveway and in our back door. Bucky was standing right inside like he'd been listening at the screen. "What happened?" he said, like I'd escaped from a prison or something.

"Nothing," I said, 'cause I didn't want to think about Mrs. Gale standing there crying.

"Think she'll call my mom?"

"Quit worrying about your stupid mom," I said.

I went past Buck and into the kitchen to get a Popsicle, but I could see Mom hadn't got back from the store yet. I thought maybe Dad wasn't home from the radio station, but then I heard him in the living room, snapping the newspaper like he always does, folding it back in half, then in half again so it would sit on his lap when he crossed his legs.

"Where's the Popsicles?" Bucky said, coming in behind me.

"Mom's not back yet," I said. I went and stood in the kitchen door. "Dad, when's Mom gonna be home?"

Like he was still reading the paper Dad said, "I don't know," then I heard him get up off the chair. He came into the kitchen with the paper and a can of beer. "Hi, Bucky," he said.

"Hi," Bucky said, not looking at him.

"Where have you boys been?"

"Out playing ball," I said, then I remembered we'd left our stuff outside. "Hey, Buck, we left our stuff out by the fence."

Buck looked at me kind of funny. "What fence?"

I said, "Right out back, by, uh..." and then I knew what he was thinking. "You know."

"Oh, yeah," Buck said. "We better get it."

He headed for the door and I went after him, but Dad said, "What are you boys up to?" When I turned around Dad was smiling a little but I could see in his eyes he was thinking more than smiling. I almost never get away with anything when he does that. Behind me I heard Bucky go out and close the door real soft instead of letting it slap like it usually does.

"Nothing," I said.

"You stay out of Mrs. Gale's trees, okay?" he said.

"Yeah," I said, then I backed up to the door and went out, Dad watching me the whole way.

Bucky was right outside like he'd been listening at the screen. "You get in trouble?" he asked.

"I don't think so," I said. "I wish I knew how he knows what I'm doin' all the time."

Bucky bit his lip like he does and I saw purple on his teeth. I looked at my fingers and Bucky's fingers and they were purple too. I held my hands up to Bucky.

Bucky looked at his purple fingers. "You think your dad's mad?"

"No," I said. "He'd a got mad already if he was mad."

We walked around the front of our garage, then cut back through the space between it and Mrs. Gale's garage. Bucky tried licking his fingers and I did too, but I couldn't taste anything and the purple didn't come off at all. I picked up my bat and Bucky grabbed his ball and glove, and then just to hear the sound I gave the fence a smack with my bat.

It rattled a bit and then Mrs. Gale screamed "Oh, my God!" It was so loud I looked up to see if she was standing on the garage roof.

Bucky yelled, "Nice goin'!" and ran back between the garages. I ran after him and when I came out the other side I saw Mrs. Gale come out in front of her house and run over to our front porch.

Bucky was hiding inside the back door. I ran right past him into the living room to tell Dad I hadn't done anything, but Dad wasn't there. Bucky ran up behind me, and right when I tried to run up the stairs Mrs. Gale opened the front door and came in so fast she almost knocked us down. She grabbed my arms and squeezed them so hard I thought she was gonna smash them. "Where's your father!" she yelled.

"We didn't go in your yard!" I yelled back. "I promise! I hit the fence with my bat!"

"I didn't do anything!" Bucky yelled. "I didn't!"

I didn't hear Dad coming down the steps until Mrs. Gale saw him and let go of me. She ran over to Dad and grabbed his arms like she'd been grabbing mine and said, "We had a terrible fight! I went to the store!"

"We didn't go in her yard again, Dad!" I yelled. "We didn't!"

"Don't call my mom!" Bucky yelled, looking like he was about to cry.

Mrs. Gale's voice was shaking. "I can't wake

Hillary," she said. "I think she took something."

Dad looked at Mrs. Gale, then came over and bent down right in front of me. Real fast he said, "I want you and Bucky to stay in the house until your mother gets home. I don't want you to do anything you're not supposed to do or get into anything or cause any trouble, you understand me?" He looked like he wasn't kidding more than I could ever remember him not kidding before.

"Yes," I said.

"You tell your mom Hillary's sick and I took her to the hospital, okay?"

"Okay," I said, then he and Mrs. Gale went out the front door in a hurry. I wanted to shut the door behind him but I thought maybe I wasn't supposed to do that so I decided I'd stand right where I was until Mom came home.

Pretty soon I heard Mrs. Gale again, outside. "It's my fault," she was saying. "It's my fault."

I went to the living room window and Bucky came too, and we saw Dad carrying Hillary out to Mrs. Gale's car. Hillary's head was bouncing up and down and Dad had a hard time getting her in the back seat. Mrs. Gale got in back with Hillary and Dad got in front and started Mrs. Gale's car. He looked right at me for a second, then backed the car down the drive and drove away.

"What do you think's wrong with her?" I said.

Bucky put his arms on the window sill and put his chin on his hands. "I don't know," he said. "I feel sick too."

We stayed by the window awhile, then went out

on the front porch to wait for Mom so we wouldn't do anything wrong in the house. When Mom got home I told her what Dad had said. She got so upset she gave me and Bucky a whole Popsicle each instead of splitting one in half like she usually does. When she tried to call the hospital she had Megan on her hip the whole time, and that made me think again about Megan losing her finger. I didn't remember much about it, but Mom cried about it for a long time, and showing her I still had all my own fingers didn't help.

Dad got home after dinner, which was hot dogs because Mom said she was too worried about Hillary to cook anything else. After he talked to Mom a bit I asked him what was wrong with Hillary and he said she'd made herself pretty sick, but she was gonna be okay, as long as she didn't make herself sick again. Mom told him not to say that and Dad said something about putting his head in the sand, and then I didn't understand anything they were saying so me and Bucky went into the living room.

I looked out the window at Mrs. Gale's house and there weren't any lights on. "Mom says Mrs. Gale's gonna stay overnight at the hospital with Hillary," I said.

"So?" Bucky said.

"So maybe the mulberries are ripe higher up in the tree."

I looked at Bucky and he looked back at me and smiled. "It's gonna be dark soon," he said.

I yelled, "We're goin' out to play!" and we were almost out the front door when Dad yelled, "Forget it!" I heard Mom say something to him, and he said something back, then Mom came to the front door.

"After I put Megan to bed how about we have popcorn and pop, and play some cards?" she said.

Bucky got a big smile on his face and said, "Okay."

Mom turned back to the kitchen and said, "Honey, we'd like you to play too."

In the kitchen Dad said, "I'm tired, okay?"

Mom said, "Dear, I think tonight it would be good for us to all spend some time together, if you know what I mean."

I didn't know what she meant, but Dad must have because after a minute he came out and said, "Who wants to help make popcorn?"

We played cards and ate popcorn and drank pop until it was real late, and Bucky and me won a bunch of the fish games, but not as much at rummy. Mom finally made us go to bed when Dad fell asleep on the couch and started snoring. I thought he was tired from having to carry Hillary out to the car, but Mom said he'd just had a long day.

Mom tucked Bucky into the cot in my room, then she tucked me in my bed. "Don't worry about Hillary," she said. "I think she's going to be all right."

"Okay," I said, even though I hadn't been worrying about Hillary. Mom gave us both a kiss and paused at the door and said maybe we'd make French toast in the morning.

After she closed the door Bucky and I talked awhile about whether anyone would tell his mom about us getting caught in the mulberry tree. I told him I didn't think anybody would remember that part, what with Hillary getting sick, and pretty soon he was breathing like he does when I know he's asleep and not just pretending.

I crawled out from under the covers and looked out the open window next to the end of my bed. There weren't any lights on next door, except for the little orange dial of Hillary's alarm clock, which was glowing in the window of her room. I leaned on the windowsill and listened to the leaves rustling in the big elm out back and in the big maple in front. The cool air felt good and I could see stars all over the sky.

After a while I got back under the covers and right then the phone rang in Mrs. Gale's house. It kept ringing a long time, and when it finally stopped it seemed like the whole neighborhood had gotten quiet, and I couldn't hear the trees anymore.

I thought about Mrs. Gale crying with the apples in her hands, and I pulled the blankets up close. Right before I fell asleep I saw Dad looking at me through the windshield of Mrs. Gale's car, like he wanted to tell me something.

THE GORILLA

~ June ~

School had been out about two weeks and it was getting pretty boring on my block. Most of the other kids in the neighborhood were on summer trips with their families, and Bucky'd been sick at home all week. I didn't even have Megan to play with because she was staying up at Grandma's for a few days.

While Mom and Dad were at work during the day I got to stay with Mrs. Wibbley down the street. I liked her because I could tell her I was going out to play and she didn't care what I did as long as I was back before Mom or Dad came to get me.

It was hard thinking of things to do all by myself, though, and most of the things I'd come up with hadn't been that great. I'd adopted two cats and a dog, and a squirrel that died, but I had to give them all back, except for the squirrel. I'd started a secret club that nobody else could join unless they gave me a quarter, but there wasn't anybody around I could tell about it. I'd also climbed some tall trees and scouted places to hide when somebody was after me, because about the only thing left to do was bug some kids I didn't like down on the next street. They're always dressed real nice and they aren't allowed to get dirty.

One day I thought about getting a paper route until Mrs. Wibbley told me how much she hated it when her paper was late or wet or not on the porch. Then she told me about all the paperboys she'd had and I almost wished I was back in school. Mrs. Wibbley's nice like I said, but it takes forever to get out of her house when she starts talking about something.

Anyway, Mom and Dad were getting ready for a costume party down the block at the Logans', and I was getting ready to spend the night at Mrs. Wibbley's because it was one of those parties where they weren't sure when they would get home, but whenever it was it was going to be late. I tried to get Mom to have the party at our house, because then I'd have things to do like sneak pretzels, but she said she was glad it was somebody else doing the work.

One good thing was that Mrs. Wibbley always made me pancakes for breakfast, and she always had real maple syrup. She even tried to make animals out of the batter 'cause I told her that's what Grandma does, but all the things she made just ran together. After a while I quit trying to guess what they were, and a while after that she went back to round ones.

While Mom was messing with her costume I finished the fish sticks and salad she made for dinner, then I put some comic books and pajamas in my bag and forgot my toothbrush because Mrs. Wibbley always has a new toothbrush if you forget your own. I tried to get out of the house by yelling goodbye but Mom ran after me and asked if I had everything, including my toothbrush. I told her the war paint she had on her face didn't look like it should and I could fix it if she wanted me to. She gave me a big kiss and I wiped it off, then she gave me a big hug and told me to be careful like I was going lion hunting or something. Mrs. Wibbley lives four houses down on our side of the street.

By the time I got there I had a couple of good rocks for me and some flowers for Mrs. Wibbley. She likes flowers and thinks I bring them from my house so I don't say anything about it. They were peonies and they smelled great, but every time I thought I'd flicked off the last big black ant another popped out somewhere to see what was going on. When I got to Mrs. Wibbley's I sat on her front steps, flicking ants off and looking for more, but I pulled the peonies apart so bad I finally tossed them under her front porch and stomped on the ants that were running for cover.

From Mrs. Wibbley's porch I could see the Logans' house a few yards down on the other side of the street. They've got a fence around their patio and there's all kinds of bushes to hide in there, but the Logans don't have any kids so it's usually out of bounds when we're playing.

I could see some lamps strung up around the patio, and Mr. Logan was putting bowls and things on card tables, and setting up chairs and laughing and yelling back into the house. He messed with the barbecue for a minute and got a puff of smoke in his face, then he tried flipping a spatula and dropped it. When he picked it up he looked back at the house to see if anyone saw him.

Mr. Logan went inside and I waited for him to come back out but he didn't. I thought about getting some more peonies, but then I noticed a line of little red ants carrying off the black ones I'd smashed.

I followed the red ants along a crack in the sidewalk to a little pile of sand by the steps. Ants were coming and going along the same path, running into each other and disappearing into a hole in the sand. I didn't want to tell Mrs. Wibbley I was there yet so I got down and watched them up close. They didn't seem to know where they were going but they all went the same way just the same.

A little blue dragonfly, so skinny you could almost see through it, landed on the sidewalk by the line of red ants. It looked as big as an airplane compared to the ants, and got me thinkin' about the big dragonflies I'd seen around, and the butterflies too. I jumped up and ran into Mrs. Wibbley's house and it seemed like I had to yell forever before she found me.

She didn't have a bug net but we made a good one out of a coat hanger and some green screen she had in her basement. I wanted pins and a board to stick the bugs on, but she gave me a jar with holes punched in the lid and made me promise not to kill anything except flies and mosquitoes.

I got out the back door before she could make me taste the pickled beets she was eating, and headed down the alley to the tracks. A train had spilled some grain down there a few days before, and the day after that it rained so the spill was getting real rotten and smelly. The weeds were thick there too, and the ditches were filled with scum water so it seemed like the best place to look for dragonflies or anything else I could catch.

On the way down the alley I saw a lot of bees and flies, and tons of little white butterflies and little yellow butterflies, but nothing worth chasing too hard. At a garden I picked a thick red rhubarb stalk and broke off the big green poison leaf. The first bite was so sour I almost threw it away, but I kept gnawing on the stalk and it tasted better and better.

The weeds were thick going down the hill to the tracks. I walked over the scummy ditch on an old railroad tie and all the frogs nearby got real quiet. I looked up and down the tracks but nothing was going on so I walked over to the spilled grain.

The pile was pretty big, with most of it right between the rails. It looked like lumpy brown oatmeal with flies all over it. It smelled terrible, and when I threw a rock into the middle that turned it up a little and made it smell worse. The flies buzzed around mad and loud for a minute before going back to eating.

My mouth got so puckered from the rhubarb that it started to hurt, so I stopped sucking on the stalk and pulled some of the strings out of the skin. There were only a couple little dragonflies sitting on the grain so I walked over to one of the ditch ponds and the frogs nearby got quiet again. I sat on an old torn-up tie that didn't have too much tar on it, and after a while the frogs started croakin' like I wasn't there.

I tossed what was left of the rhubarb behind me and sat completely still, watching the weeds and the water and keeping track of all the bugs that came and went. I don't know how long I was there but I lost count almost right away. There were tons of bees going through the weeds and as many little dragonflies as you could want, and even a few bugs skittering around on the water in the ditch, but there weren't any big dragonflies anywhere.

A block away two big kids waded through the weeds and out onto the tracks under the Summit Street bridge. The bridge is neat because it's made of real wood and looks like the little plastic one Dad helped me make for my train set. It's also easy to climb, but we never go all the way up 'cause it's pretty high, and the pigeons swoop around, and everything up there is covered with bird poo. It's scary when a car goes over, too, 'cause you can feel everything move, and once in a while something pops or cracks and it seems like the whole thing is going to fall down.

I heard a little sound and saw the big kids were shooting a BB gun up at the pigeons. I thought I'd seen the kid that wasn't doing the shooting, and I'd heard stories about him getting in trouble. He came around school sometimes after it let out, and he and his friends ganged up on anyone that didn't get home fast enough. I watched them for a while and they kept grabbing the gun from each other and shooting at the birds, but I didn't see any birds that looked like they'd been hit.

I got thinking about the dragonflies again and I couldn't stop daydreaming, and pretty soon I was lookin' up at the sky for ten-foot dragonflies. I knew there weren't any but I couldn't quit thinking about them so I looked for a place to hide if one showed up. I looked at the weeds and watched the yellow jackets and the bumblebees working on all of the flowers, then I looked up again because I didn't hear the frogs anymore.

The big kids were walking down the tracks toward me, shooting at everything whether it was moving or not. They spotted me about the same time I saw them and pointed the gun at me. I grabbed the net, ducked into the weeds and climbed up the hill to the end of the street. I could hear them yelling and shooting but I didn't look back until I was behind a telephone pole at the top of the hill.

When I finally looked they were standing by the ditch trying to shoot frogs, but they weren't quiet enough to get the frogs singing again. The kid who didn't have the gun was gettin' mad at the kid I knew for wasting shots. The kid with the gun picked something up and threw it into the air. He shot at it and missed, then I saw what it was before it smashed on a rail and I heard the glass break.

"You stupid jerk!" I yelled, then I ran down the street for Mrs. Wibbley's. When I looked back they were standing by the phone pole fighting over the gun. I stayed on the wrong side of the street 'cause I didn't want them to know where I was going, and I kept looking back until they started wrestling and slid down the hill out of sight.

I thought I could still hear them yelling at each other, but I kept walking and the yelling turned into music coming from the Logans' party. I wasn't thinking about bugs anymore since the jar was busted, but it turned out the net Mrs. Wibbley helped me make was pretty good for whackin' the heads off dandelions. Then, right when I stopped to count the heads still stuck in the net, a Monarch butterfly landed on a bush in front of me.

It fluttered its wings a few times, then spread them out wide and stood still. It wasn't a big dragonfly but it was better than nothing, so I shook the dandelions out of the net and crept around behind it. When I was close I crouched down, got the net ready, then dove for it and missed.

As the butterfly flew across the Conleys' front yard I got a few more swipes at it, then it flew back over their garage. I thought I'd lose it having to go around, but it came down again right when I got to the other side. I got in a few more good swings, and I kept swinging, but a butterfly's hard to catch because they don't ever just fly straight.

I got close a couple times, but then I had to duck under a fence that had grapes growing all over it, and when I came out the other side the butterfly was headed back to the street. I cut through some bushes that scratched me pretty good, then I ran straight into a tree because a lady in a leopard skin jumped in front of me, screaming at the top of her lungs and scaring me to death.

She had long blonde hair and was screeching like a rabid dog was after her. She ran across the yard and into a bunch of bushes and disappeared. I stood there thinking she might come back, then I turned around to see what scared her. All I could see for a minute was a big black wall of fur, then I looked up and there was a giant gorilla staring down at me. I screamed and backed up, but the gorilla came after me with his red eyes and white fangs and I thought for sure I was dead.

The gorilla growled real loud and tried to grab me but I jumped back into the bushes the woman had run through. I landed between two little pine trees and ducked down, then crawled behind another bush and spun around. At the edge of the bushes the gorilla's feet moved toward me so I scooted back even more until a branch poked me in the back and I couldn't go any farther. I could hear the gorilla rustling around and I could see the bushes moving, then his feet came close again and I closed my eyes.

When I finally opened them again the gorilla was gone and I heard talking real close by. I heard the lady scream again, then the gorilla growled, then people laughed and it sounded like they were right behind me. I turned around real quiet and as soon as I saw it I knew I was looking at the Logans' patio fence.

I crawled up and looked through one of the square holes where there weren't any flowers growing on the other side. The lanterns were on and a lot of people were there, wearing all kinds of costumes. The lady who was screaming turned out to be Mrs. Logan. I was pretty sure Mr. Logan was the gorilla but I couldn't see him so I decided to wait to be sure. I saw Mom in her Indian costume, and her war paint was better. She was talking with one of her and Dad's friends, but mostly I couldn't tell who anybody was. Some of them I couldn't even tell what they were supposed to be.

The music started again and a few people danced, but mostly there were just little groups of people all talking at once. Over the song I heard Dad's voice but I couldn't see him. "Hey!" he yelled, and I thought for a minute he was looking for me. "Do you know your monkey peed in my martini?" I looked around for a monkey but then Dad said, "No, but if you hum a few bars," and everybody laughed. I didn't get it, but Dad says a lot of things I don't get.

The gorilla appeared again and went over to a bar that had been set up at the back of the patio. A guy dressed like a baseball player was behind the bar and gave the gorilla a drink. The gorilla said something and pointed under the bar and the baseball player ducked down, then came up with a jar of olives. He opened the jar and dropped an olive in the gorilla's glass.

The gorilla lifted the glass to take a sip, then re-membered he had to take his head off first. While he was doing that Dad walked over and took a pair of weird-looking pliers out of the long white coat he was wearing. He'd told me he was dressed like a special doctor but I couldn't remember what kind. The only thing I remembered was Mom hit him when he said it.

The gorilla finally pulled his head off and it was Mr. Logan like I thought. While he was putting the gorilla head on the bar Dad snuck Mr. Logan's olive with the pliers, then stepped back. Mr. Logan picked up his drink and almost took a sip, then noticed the olive was missing. Dad woulda got away with it but the guy in the baseball uniform laughed and Mr. Logan figured out what was going on. When Dad showed him the olive in the pliers Mr. Logan covered his glass like he didn't want it back and everybody laughed again.

In the bushes around me I could hear a cricket, and when I looked up past the lanterns I saw a firefly. I looked for my net until I spotted it, but when I looked back at the patio Mr. Logan was talking to Dad and pointing at the bushes. Dad looked like he could see me right through the fence, and he had that look he gets when he's going to tell me something whether I want to hear it or not.

I scrambled out as fast as I could but I got my pants caught for a second on an old branch. If I'd been smart I would've left my net lying right where it was, but I felt dumb about the jar and I didn't want to go back to Mrs. Wibbley's and have her think I lost everything.

I picked up the net and ran around a tree and across the Logans' front yard. There weren't any cars coming, which was good 'cause I didn't want to have to stop out there in the open, but it didn't matter because right then Dad yelled, "Hold it!"

I stopped at the curb, stepping down and up while he walked over. I picked the last of the dandelions out of the net and looked up at him, but with the patio lanterns behind him I couldn't see his face. I looked up at the sky and it was getting dark in the east, and suddenly there were fireflies everywhere.

Dad turned me around, looking at the tar on my pants and the rips in my clothes. He reached down and pulled some dry pine needles out of my hair. "Looks like you've been busy," he said.

I held up the net to make sure he could see it. "I've been huntin' bugs," I said. I wished I had some to show him but all I had was the net with dandelion bits stuck in it.

"Do you know what time it is?" he said.

I tried to think of the answer but all I knew was it was getting dark and I should've been at Mrs. Wibbley's. While I was trying to think what to say a street-light flickered on behind me and I could see Dad's face. He looked scary in his doctor clothes, and I could see the handles of the weird pliers sticking out of his coat pocket. He was staring at me and I didn't know what to do, then all of a sudden I got a thought that came out before I had a chance to think it over. "Hum a few bars," I said.

He didn't seem happy to hear me say that, which was when I remembered I didn't know what it meant. I got worried for a minute that it was like swearing, or maybe worse.

I heard Mom laugh nearby and saw her on the lawn standing with a couple people. One of them said something to Dad about a chip off a block and they all laughed again. Dad looked at them, then back at me, and said, "As your physician, I suggest you get to Mrs. Wibbley's without delay to prevent further complica-tions." It was one of those things Dad said where I didn't understand it but I knew what he meant.

He gave me a slap on the butt that was softer than I thought it was gonna be. "Look both ways," he said, and I could feel him standing there, watching me look up and down the street until my head almost fell off. I didn't look back until I was halfway to Mrs. Wibbley's house.

When I got there I hid behind one of the porch posts and peeked back at the Logans'. Mom and Dad were back on the patio, and when a song started up Dad pulled Mom over and they danced slow and close together. Mr. Logan had his gorilla head back on and was dancing with a lady who was dressed like she was in the army.

I looked up and down the street and every yard was full of fireflies. There were more of them than I could see stars in the sky. It was cool and still and you could hear the music from the Logans', and the low sky behind the lanterns was bright and blue.

I kept watching the fireflies, and after a while I could tell where one was gonna flash next. Sometimes they went a different way, but a lot of the time you could really tell. I watched them until I heard Mrs. Wibbley inside, opening up the couch.

I opened the front screen but I didn't go in. "Mrs. Wibbley!" I yelled. "I need another jar!"

MEGAN

~ *July* ~

It was the Fourth of July and it was the same as always only worse. Mom and Dad dragged us off to our picnic out in the country, where I was getting bitten to death 'cause nobody remembered the bug spray. My little sister, Megan, bugged me every five minutes about when the fireworks were, until I told her I didn't know if there were going to be any fireworks 'cause last year one fell in the crowd and blew up and killed a hundred people.

She said it didn't happen and grabbed her hand where her little finger was missing. I said it did and it blew all the people to bits. She started crying and ran over to Mom and I went back to watching some squirrels chase each other up and down the side of a tree. I wondered about their feet and what kept them from falling off, and it seemed like they should anyway as fast as they were going.

"I thought you weren't going to tease your sister about her finger anymore."

I turned around and Dad was standing over me like another tree. Megan was sitting by the grill on Mom's lap, watching me.

"I didn't say anything about her finger," I said, looking back at the squirrels. They were peeking out from behind the tree, watching me. Dad walked around the way I was looking and crouched down in front of me. The squirrels ran up into the tree, taking little peeks on the way.

"She said you told her she'd get blown up at the fireworks."

"She's lying."

"Who's lying?"

"She was bugging me," I said, looking down at nothing. "Make her stop bugging me and I won't tease her anymore."

"Son, you won't tease her because I told you not to tease her. I don't care how much she bugs you. Do you understand me?"

"That's not fair! How come she gets to bug me and I don't get to bug her?"

The way he was looking at me I thought he was going to hit me he was so mad. "Have you ever thought what it would be like to lose one of your own fingers?" he said, all quiet and angry. "You think something like that can't happen to you?"

I sat on my hands. I got sick thinking about it.

He stared at me and I looked away again. Mom called him and said the hamburgers needed turning. Dad said, "You think about it," and walked back over to the grill.

I kept sitting on my hands. At first I could feel all the clumps of dirt and blades of grass they were touching, but then they got tingly and I could feel them going to sleep. The squirrels went back to running around the tree, and I thought how they'd fall off for sure if they didn't have all their toes.

Mom called and said it was time to eat. I yelled back that I wasn't hungry and Dad yelled back that I was. I got off my hands and put them in my pockets, and on the way over to the blanket the feeling started coming back to my fingers, stinging and burning.

*   *   *

The ride home was hot and I kept scratching my bug bites and trying not to think about having to go to the hospital to get my finger cut off, which is what happened to Megan after Mom smashed it. I kept sitting up to look out the front window, making sure we were going home.

Megan said, "When are the fireworks?"

Mom said, "Not till dark," like the hundred other times Megan had asked.

"When's that?" she said.

"When the sun goes down," I said.

"When's that?"

I could see Dad looking at me in the rear-view mirror. "When the stars come out," I said.

"When's that?"

When I push you out a window and you land on your head, I thought. "Bed time," I said.

"No, I want to see! Mom, I want to see the fireworks! You said!"

Dad gave me a look like I did something wrong and Mom told Megan she'd get to see the fireworks. I was looking at Megan's hand where her pinkie was missing, and my pinkie kept hurting right where hers was gone. I thought about all the times I'd held up my hands and wiggled my pinkies and I felt bad about it.

Megan was little when it got crushed so she didn't remember, but I could still hear her screaming and see her with a big bandage on her hand like a mitten. Mom held on to Megan all the time after that. She even had Dad throw out the chair she scooted back on Megan's hand 'cause she hated it so much.

When we got home I went up to my room and shut the door. I played with some green clay for a while, rolling it into a ball, then into a log, then back into a ball. I thought about Dad and I didn't think he'd ever take me to the hospital to get one of my fingers cut off, but then I remembered the time in the basement when he broke my baseball bat. He told me he'd been trying to kill a rat, but when Mom caught me standing in the washing machine with Bucky's slingshot she said there weren't any rats and Dad got mad at the bat after he tripped over it.

I rolled the clay into a log again and broke off a piece as long as my pinkie. I tried pressing it on my knuckle but it wouldn't stay. I didn't have any pink clay anyway so I knew they'd figure out it was a fake at the hospital.

I practiced doing things without using my pinkie and it didn't seem too hard, except the first couple times I tried to tie my shoes. I tried writing without it, and playing jacks, and throwing a ball, and I didn't think I'd miss it too much, and I thought maybe it'd even get me out of music lessons if Dad made me take them like he said he was going to.

*   *   *

When we drove back downtown Mom said she wondered why I was being so quiet and Dad said she shouldn't look at a horse in the mouth, which I didn't understand. I told her I was just thinking, then Megan said people got blown up last year and she didn't want to get blown up. Dad pulled the car over all of a sudden and turned around and looked at me.

"What's the matter with you?"

"I didn't say anything!"

Mom said, "What have you been telling her about the fireworks?"

"I just told her about last year when that firework fell in the crowd and blew up."

Dad let out a snort and slapped the back of the front seat. "It didn't blow up in the crowd! Who told you that?" He turned even more so he could look at Megan behind him. "Megan, nobody blew up. One man burned his hand throwing an unexploded firework in the river. Okay? You won't get hurt, honey."

"They go boom," said Megan.

"Boom makes the pretty colors, Megan," Mom said.

Dad pulled back on the street and I got nervous when he turned and drove down the hill toward the river. On the bluff on the other side I could see the hospital towers sticking out of the trees. I remembered Megan going there, and the blood on her shirt. "We aren't going to the hospital are we?" I said, playing with the door handle and trying to look out the side window to see how fast the car was going.

Dad said no and Mom asked him what I was talking about and Dad said he didn't have any idea. I didn't feel better until Dad parked and shut off the car, which is when I started thinking about what I was gonna do to Bucky for telling me a firework blew up in the crowd and killed a guy.

Mom and Dad got the blankets out of the trunk and I walked over to the edge of the river to see if anything was floating by. Dad yelled for me and when I looked he was carrying Megan on his shoulders. Mom and Dad and Megan followed the other people along the river to City Park. I walked along the riverbank and counted ducks as they jumped away from me into the water.

I kept looking for Bucky and his mom so I could watch the fireworks with him, but I didn't see them. Mom and Dad stopped to talk with some people for a minute, then decided we'd stay on the far side of the river 'cause Megan was still scared about getting blown up.

I told Megan nothing would happen and she forgot about it while we played with some sparklers. I spelled my name in the air, then I tried to spell "Kill Bucky" but the sparkler ran out. Megan ran around holding the sparkler behind her and screaming like it was after her.

More and more people kept coming until it looked like everyone in Summit was there. Across the river the grass in front of the university auditorium was filled with blankets, and a bunch of kids were running along the river bank, their sparklers reflecting in the water.

The sky overhead was dark blue when the warning shots went off, telling everyone the fireworks were about to start. The first one made me jump and I could hear it echo along the bluffs up and down the river. Megan screamed and hid on Mom's lap. I lay down on my back on the extra blanket and watched the puffs of smoke from the warning shots drift over my head.

The sky got darker and darker, and after a while I couldn't make out the people on the other side of the river. Up the river, a police car was sitting on the bridge to the park with its lights flashing. That meant no more cars could cross so I knew it was about time.

A couple minutes later, down in the park on the other side of the bridge, I could see something glowing and burning on the ground. I could hear people cheering as it burned bright, then died down. I saw the same thing every year, but I never knew what it was 'cause we never sat down in the park itself. I thought about asking Dad to take me over to the park, but I didn't want him to remember me so I didn't.

I was looking at the sky, counting the stars I could see when the first firework blew up in front of them. It was blue and gold and fell like a splash from a puddle. I jumped and Megan and other little kids around us screamed. When the echo stopped I could hear the crowd all along the river, ooohing real quiet.

I looked at the park and saw a flash. I watched the tail of a firework shooting into the sky, then the sound of it came a moment later. I lost the tail in the stars, then the firework blew up like a red and green water-fall. The sparks reflected on the river as they fell.

I'd forgotten how loud fireworks were when they

blew up, and how you could feel them in your body. I plugged my ears when one blew up blue and white and a bunch of bright flashes went off as it fell down. The flashes were real loud, and I looked over at Megan and she was covering her ears too. She hid her face against Mom, then looked, then hid again, like she didn't like it either way.

I watched more fireworks go off, and after a while I left my fingers in my ears because the noise kept making me jump. There were a few quiet ones shaped like big comets with long orange tails, but then another one would go off all bright with loud explosions that went right through me.

There were huge fireworks, like giant dandelions, so high they seemed like they were going to fall right on us before they disappeared. There were red ones and blue ones, and green and white, and some that changed colors as they fell. I got pretty good at following them on the way up, but sometimes I'd lose them and it seemed like forever before they exploded. Every once in a while the sparks would fall all the way back down into the park and Megan would scream and hide her face.

Each time a firework lit up the sky I could see gray smoke trails floating over my head, like giant spiders somebody smashed with a shoe. I showed them to Megan but they scared her more and she hid her eyes again. Dad said to leave her alone and Mom said something to him that I didn't hear because another firework exploded and I stuck my fingers back in my ears.

Whenever they stopped shooting to reload I could see another glow in the park. I didn't mind 'cause it gave me a chance to take my fingers out of my ears, which were getting sore. I watched Megan then, and even when it got real quiet she never let go of Mom's shirt with the hand where her finger was missing.

When they began shooting fireworks off again one blew up bright blue and lit up some low clouds I hadn't seen before on the other side of the park. The clouds glowed for a second, but when the firework died they were gone. When the next firework exploded I could tell the clouds were getting closer and bigger, and with the next one they began to look like mountains.

The clouds kept growing and glowing in different colors, the fireworks making shadows on their faces like valleys and caves. I kept waiting for them to blow right over but they just got bigger and bigger and made the fireworks look small.

When they shot off all the fireworks at the end like they always do there were clouds all across the sky. Lying on my back it was like looking up the side of the tallest cliff in the world. The colors flashed across the clouds and the explosions sounded like a war.

Everyone was clapping and cheering at the end, when so many fireworks went off at once it made the insides of the clouds glow like they were on fire. I was looking straight up and I had to close my eyes to keep from feeling like I was falling off the earth.

*   *   *

Megan talked about the fireworks all the way back to the car. I wanted her to shut up, but when she fell asleep on the ride home it was even worse. Nobody said anything then, and I could see Dad looking at me in the rear-view mirror when car lights flashed on his face.

I'd pretty much decided Dad wasn't going to take me to the hospital, but I kept watch out the window anyway. I got nervous again when we didn't go on any of the streets I knew, but then we came around a corner and I saw John's Grocery up the block. Dad pulled in the parking lot and Mom went in to get milk for the morning, and Dad told her to get some potato salad too.

I wanted to say something to Dad, but I didn't want him looking at me anymore so I pretended to be asleep. I closed my eyes until I could barely see out and watched him watching for Mom. When he got tired of turning around he moved the rear-view mirror so he could see when she was coming. He turned on the radio real quiet.

The music started off soft, but by the time we got home it was loud and kind of scary, like the Sorcerer's Apprentice. Mom took the groceries in and Dad carried Megan. She grabbed onto him in her sleep and he kissed her hand where her finger was missing.

I followed them upstairs and went to my room. It was cold and dark and down the hall I could hear Megan crying. Dad came in and yelled at me for making Megan cry, then he got out my busted bat and hit it against the floor like a drum. I yelled for Mom and she ran in and took my hand and squeezed it so hard I couldn't feel it. I looked down and my little finger turned green and fell off and I yelled but nobody heard me over the drum.

*   *   *

I woke up and rain was blowing through the window by my bed, soaking the covers. A clap of thunder shook the house and I jumped. I curled into a ball away from the wet part of the bed and rubbed my hand to get the feeling back into it. I kept feeling my pinkie to make sure it was still there.

The lightning was so bright I could see it even with the blanket pulled up over my head. The thunder was getting closer and every time it went off it made the glass in the windows buzz. It felt like the thunder and lightning were right in the room, right over my bed.

The feeling came back to my fingers and I decided right then that I'd run off and live with Bucky before I'd let anybody cut off my finger. I got real mad at Dad for breaking my bat, then the thunder stopped for a minute and I could still hear Megan crying.

I pulled the covers off my head and Megan's crying stopped, then it started again with another flash of lightning. I plugged my ears until the thunder rolled away, then I listened again and I could hear her crying like she does when she's scared of a big dog or doesn't want to go to bed. I heard her call for Mom, and in another flash of lightning I saw her walking down the hall with her stuffed lobster. She was crying, and when the thunder hit she screamed.

I got out of bed and the wind and rain got me pretty good. I wasn't wearing pajamas and the rain was cold when it hit me, and colder with the wind blowing. I tried turning on my light but it didn't work. I went out and tried the hall light but it didn't work either and I couldn't see Megan anywhere.

I went back in my room and tried closing the window but it was stuck and I got soaked. It seemed like the thunder and lightning were right over the house, and between the house shaking and the windows buzzing I thought I could still hear Megan crying for Mom. I stuffed my blanket in the window as good as I could.

I decided to go to Mom and Dad's room, but right then something went *tzt!* in my ears, then there was the brightest flash of lightning I ever saw. It seemed like the light came through the walls and I couldn't see anything at all for a minute. While I was trying to think what the funny sound was the thunder hit like a bomb, the sound going through me like a thousand fireworks all at once.

I felt along my wall until I got out in the hall, and by the time my eyes got used to the dark again I'd gone past Mom and Dad's room all the way to the top of the stairs. There weren't any lights on downstairs so I went back to Mom and Dad's room and looked in. When lightning flashed again I could see Megan curled up on the bed, crying.

When the thunder came it was way, way off and sounded like it was in a jar. I went in and the lightning flashed and I could see Megan crying but I could barely hear her. I didn't hear the next thunder at all but I felt it going through me and shaking the floor.

Megan looked up and saw me and I could tell she yelled, "Where's Mommy!" but I couldn't hear her. She looked scared worse than I'd ever seen her, and it made me worry about where Mom was too.

I turned to go out in the hall but Megan jumped off the bed and grabbed me. Her hands were as cold as the rain and I felt her tears when she pressed up against me. I wanted to find Mom but I was shaking from the cold and my teeth were chattering so I sat on the edge of the bed with Megan and pulled a blanket up around us. A rumble of thunder went through me and Megan squeezed me and it was hard to breathe.

I wanted to yell for Mom but all of a sudden I was tired. I pulled the blanket over Megan and around my head and just sat there all wet, too tired even to scratch the bug bites that were itching me. I closed my eyes and watched the flashes of lightning through my eyelids and felt the thunder getting farther away. I put my arm around Megan to get her to stop shaking and crying on me.

Lightning flashed, and it took a minute before I realized it didn't get dark again. I opened my eyes and closed them again in a real hard squint. All the lights in the bedroom were on, and in the hall, and it stung.

I looked out the door and saw Mom go past toward Megan's room, then Megan started squirming around, trying to get out of the blanket and away from me. She ran to the hall as Mom came in the door and they hugged real tight. I pulled the blanket around me closer.

Mom came over carrying Megan and asked me if I was okay, but she sounded far away like she was calling on the phone from Grandma's house. I told her my bed was all wet and she went off to look, still rubbing Megan's back and carrying her like she wasn't ever going to put her down.

Dad came in the room and smiled at me. He said something about the storm, then he turned toward the closet and I couldn't see the rest of what he said. I closed my eyes so I wouldn't have to say anything, but he must have kept talking 'cause a minute later he was shaking my shoulder and I could barely hear him calling me.

I opened my eyes and he was looking right in my face like he was mad. "Don't ignore me," he said, and it sounded strange, like he was on the phone too.

"I can't hear," I said.

"And don't lie to me," he said, squeezing my shoulder like the principal does when he catches me running in the hall.

"I'm not lying!" I yelled back. "I can't hear!"

Dad said a whole bunch real fast that I didn't get, and I could tell he was mad, but it wasn't so bad with him sounding as quiet as he did. He grabbed both of my shoulders and said, "Are you listening to me?"

I felt like crying so I didn't look at him anymore, but Dad grabbed my chin and made me. "I can't hear!" I yelled. "I can't! And if you try to cut off my finger I'll run away and never come back!"

Dad said about two more words and then stopped. He turned around and Mom was standing in the door, still holding Megan against her, a hand over Megan's ear. She said something to Dad and he stood up with his head down a little. Mom asked him something and he said something and all of a sudden she was so mad I thought she was gonna throw Megan at him.

Mom came over and pulled the blanket away and rubbed her hand through my wet hair. She asked me why I couldn't hear and I said I didn't know but maybe it was the thunder. Mom looked at Dad like she looks at me when I do something really stupid, then she rubbed my arm and took my hand and we went into Megan's room.

Mom already had my pillow in there, and she helped me into bed and put Megan in beside me. She turned off the lights and sat with us a long time, rubbing my arm and running her hand through Megan's hair. Dad stood in the door once for a minute, but Mom said something without looking and he went away.

Megan curled up next to me and fell asleep, and Mom kissed me on the forehead and went out of the room. I could feel Megan taking big breaths and sighing from all the crying she'd done, but it didn't bother me 'cause I couldn't hear her and she was warm.

I don't know when I fell asleep, but before I did I thought I heard Mom and Dad talking somewhere, and I thought I could feel more thunder through the floor.

*   *   *

In the morning my ears were a lot better so Mom said I didn't have to go to the doctor, and breakfast was great 'cause we had so many waffles I almost got sick. When we were done eating Megan and I went out to catch worms that had come up where our backyard always gets a bunch of puddles. We were filling up our second soup can when Dad came out and had us come over to the back-porch steps.

He messed up my hair and put Megan on his knee

and said he was sorry about not believing I couldn't hear. He said he and Mom just wanted to make sure there wouldn't be any more teasing each other, so me and Megan promised him we wouldn't. He gave us each a big hug and told us he loved us and said to catch him some worms. Megan said she would, but I knew he didn't really want any.

I went back to the puddles but Megan grabbed Dad's arm and said she wanted a piggy-back ride. I didn't want to catch any more worms so I watched the ones we already had moving around in the foam they always make. Megan fussed but Dad said he had to go and went back in the house. When she came over she said she didn't want to catch any more worms and I didn't say anything.

The sun was lighting up the big brick house across the alley, and I could see part of a cloud over the roof. The air still felt like rain but it was okay with the sun out, and the brick house made me wish I was big with a house of my own.

Megan had her chin in her hands, and where her finger was missing it looked kind of sore and blue. I must have stared at it awhile because she saw what I was doing and moved her hands between her knees. She looked up at me and seemed scared, like during the fireworks. Not crying or anything, but scared in her eyes.

"I won't tease you, okay?" she said.

"Okay," I said.

We decided to let the worms go, then I gave her a piggy-back ride for a long time. We went all over the yard and I never got tired. Megan picked some leaves off a tree branch and stuck them in my hair, and we scared Mom at the kitchen window when Megan pretended she was trying to climb in. We even snuck next door and Megan peeked in at what Hillary and Mrs. Gale were watching on TV.

The sun came out and made the grass shine and I didn't ever want to put her down. Megan laughed and said she was big and wanted Dad to see her. I wanted Dad to see me.

THE TREE HOUSE

~ August ~

It stayed so hot all night that when me and Bucky woke up our sheets had sweat stains on them in the shapes of our bodies. You could see how Bucky'd been sleeping on the cot by the shape of his sweat, but my bed was harder to figure 'cause I'd been lying on my side. It looked kinda like I only had one leg, and Buck said it looked like a flamingo except for my head.

We put our shorts on then tried hopping all the way down to the kitchen on one foot, but Buck fell down the last two steps and cut his lip on the latch of my dad's cornet case. I'd tripped over it myself a few times until I got used to it sitting on the bottom step, which it had been for as long as I could remember.

Mom leaned out of the kitchen holding the cup of tea she always had in the morning, and asked what we were doing. I said we weren't doing anything and Bucky got up, sucking on the corner of his lip. "Did you hurt your lip, Bucky?" Mom said.

Bucky shook his head and I shook my head too, but I don't think she believed us. "Come on and get breakfast," she said. "It's gonna be another scorcher today." I got past her to the kitchen table, but she made

Buck stop and show her his lip.

"I don't need stitches, do I?" Buck said, real worried. He'd had so many stitches we didn't even try counting them anymore.

"No, you don't need stitches," Mom said. "But you do need to be a little more careful."

"I don't know how it happens," Buck said, sitting across the table from me. "I think I'm jinxed."

Mom told him she was sure he wasn't jinxed, so I didn't say anything 'cause I was pretty sure he was. Once I saw Buck ride a wheelie half a block, then when he was riding back he ran right into a parked car. He got eight stitches in his chin that time, and felt so dumb about it he told his mom he crashed doing the wheelie, which I thought was pretty smart until his mom took his bike away for two weeks.

"It seems like an awful lot of dumb stuff happens to me," Buck said, tipping his chair up on the back legs.

"Well, Bucky," Mom said, tipping his chair back down. "Maybe you only need to pay a little more attention to what you're doing."

"I do," he said. "It's the stuff I'm not paying attention to that gets me in trouble."

Mom laughed at that and got out two bowls and two boxes of cereal. "Don't feel too bad, Bucky," she said. "It happens to all of us." She laughed again and I looked at the cereal boxes and didn't want either one.

"Can we have pancakes, Mom?" I said, pushing the cereal boxes around to look at the backs.

"It's too hot to turn on the stove."

"How about French toast?"

Bucky turned the back of the boxes his way.

"I'd still have to turn on the stove."

"Oh, yeah," I said. I tried turning the boxes back again but Buck grabbed one and pulled it out of reach. I grabbed the other one but it wasn't the one I wanted if I had to have cereal, so I shoved it over to Buck's side and he shoved it back. "How about waffles?" I said.

"I'd have to turn the waffle iron on. Just eat the cereal okay? It won't kill you." Mom put the milk and sugar bowl on the table and gave me a pat on the head.

When she went to the counter to make another cup of tea I felt Buck kick me in the leg. I looked over and all I could see was the top of his head. He'd had to scoot so far down in his chair to give me a kick that he couldn't see I was looking back. When he tried kicking me again I kicked him back real hard.

"Ow," he said, sitting up real fast.

Mom looked at us and we looked back at her like we weren't doing anything. "My little angels," she said, turning and looking for something in the cupboard.

Buck gave me a dirty look which means he thinks I'm stupid, so I tried to kick him again, but all I did was smash my toes on a table leg. He thought that was pretty funny until I put my hands on the edge of the table and shoved the whole thing into his chest. He tried shoving it back but all that did was scoot his chair away from the table. I got a good laugh until I saw Mom watching us. She came over and fixed the table.

"You boys better be planning to spend a lot of time outside today," she said. She kept an eye on us until we started eating, then she got a cookbook out and turned around, reading it on the counter while she sipped her tea.

While I was sneaking more sugar for my cereal Buck pointed at the sugar spoon, then at the counter. He could see I wasn't getting it, so he pretended he was eating his hand, holding it all flat like a karate chop and chewing on the edges. When he could see I wasn't ever going to get it he climbed up on his chair, leaned across the table, and whispered in my ear.

Bucky sat back down and I looked at the toaster on the counter, then at the sugar bowl and spoon on the table, and I could even see the cinnamon up in the cupboard by Mom's head. "Can we have cinnamon toast?" I said.

Mom turned around with her arms folded, one hand holding the tea cup up to her lips. She looked at us a minute and said, "You boys may be playing outside until school starts."

"Really?" I said.

"Can we make a tepee?" Buck said.

Mom stood watching us until we started eating our cereal again. She sipped her tea and I spit out a mouthful of cereal real slow so she saw the whole thing. Bucky kept eating and staring into his bowl like he was studying for a test. "How come we can't have anything that heats up the house but you drink hot tea all the time?" I said.

Mom waited a minute, then said, "If you drink hot tea on a hot day it opens your pores and makes you feel cooler."

"Really?" I said. "Well my pores feel all closed up. How about you, Buck? Your pores need opening? Boy I sure do feel hot." I slumped in my chair and panted and wiped sweat off my forehead like I was lost in a desert. Mom kept sipping her tea until I'd run out of things to do and was half off the chair with my head hanging upside down.

"Would you like some cinnamon toast, Bucky?" Mom said.

"Okay," Buck said, sucking on his spoon and acting like he didn't care if he got any or not.

Mom stared at me until I sat up and ate my cereal, then she got the cinnamon out of the cupboard and started making the toast. I looked out the kitchen window at the backyard and it looked like it was going to be hot again, like it had been the day before, and the day before that. I looked across the alley at the back of the big house on Summit Street, and I thought I could hear their air conditioner running.

*   *   *

Bucky took another drink of water from his canteen, then screwed the cap back on real tight like he wasn't going to open it again for another hour. It was so hot though, by the time he got done tightening it he was thirsty again, and so was I just from watching him.

"How much you got left?" I said.

"It's almost gone," he said, taking another drink.

"We'll have to get down again," I said, not wanting to move 'cause of the heat.

When she finished making the cinnamon toast Mom kicked us out the door with the toast and our canteens. We decided to eat the toast in the tree house in the big elm in the backyard, so of course Bucky dropped his toast on the way up and it bounced off my head, cinnamon side down. I was still itching sugar out of my hair.

Once we got up in the tree house and finished the toast there wasn't much to do except be hot. The thick leaves kept the sun off us, but there wasn't any breeze at all. We tried pretending we were holding a fort against Indians, but then we decided Indians wouldn't be dumb enough to attack a fort when it was that hot, so we quit.

"You ever go all the way out on that branch?" Buck said, pointing at the one that held up the back half of the tree house. It was big around and went up a bit to where Dad tied the rope for the tire swing, then it kept going out real low all the way across the backyard to the alley. If you climbed on top of the swing set out past the peony bushes you could grab one of the small branches hanging off that main branch and make the whole thing bounce up and down.

"I got about five feet past the rope once, but Mom caught me," I said. "She made Dad get a ladder and get me down."

"That's not fair."

"Dad didn't think so either. You gonna do it?"

Buck looked over at me like I'd volunteered him for the army. "I ain't goin' out there!" he said, like it hadn't been his idea to talk about it in the first place.

"Well I ain't goin' out there either," I said, drinking the rest of my water. "Anyway I gotta fill my canteen."

Buck finished his real fast and said, "Me too."

We climbed back down and I made Bucky go first

'cause I was worried he might fall on me and kill me. We went to the faucet at the back of the house and let the water run till it got cold again, then filled up the canteens. We went back to the tree and I climbed up first so I wouldn't have to wait for Buck.

When Buck climbed up he said, "What do you want to do?"

"I don't know," I said. "What do you want to do?"

"Not this," Buck said, taking another long drink from his canteen.

"Yeah," I said, not taking a drink from mine, even though I could feel how cool the water was through the metal and the wet cloth cover. "Let's think of something else. It's too hot to just lie here. We'll get heat stroke and get dizzy and throw up and die."

"Yeah," Buck said, taking another long drink and screwing the lid on tight again.

"Let's swing," I said. "At least it'll make a breeze."

"Yeah," Buck said. "But first I gotta fill up my canteen again. And go to the bathroom."

I unscrewed the cap on mine and took a little drink. "You gotta sip it real slow and make it last," I said. "What if you were lost in a desert?"

"I'd have more than one if I was in the desert. And a camel. They hold lots of water."

"What if it got shot in the hump and all the water leaked out?"

"I'd hide. Then at night I'd sneak back and suck on the wet sand."

"It would all be evaporated. You'd die."

"Huh-uh," Buck said, looking at my canteen.

"Uh-huh," I said, taking another slow sip. "You'd

dry up like a raisin and somebody'd find you a hundred years later and put you in a museum."

Bucky started to argue, then all of a sudden he stopped and said he had to go the bathroom real bad. He musta been about to pee his pants, because when he finally got down he ran between our garage and Mrs. Gale's, which is where we go when we don't want to go inside.

*　　*　　*

After Bucky filled his canteen again we played a little on the tire swing, but it was too hot with both of us on it, and it was too hard to get a drink 'cause you always had to have a least one hand on the rope.

We went back past the peonies to the swing set and swung real slow in the hot air. The sun was higher but it was shining through the edge of the tree so I poured water on my head like I saw once in a movie. It felt good at first, and Buck did it too, but after a few minutes we were just wet and hot at the same time. Listening to the air conditioner in the house across the alley only made it worse.

I looked up at the big branch coming all the way out to us from the tree. "Hey, Buck," I said. "I bet we could stand on the swing set and grab those branches, then climb up and go all the way to the tree house without touching the ground."

"So?"

"Well what if the ground wasn't grass? What if it was a big ocean full of sharks? Would you swim for it?"

"Hey!" Buck said, all of a sudden. "Let's go swimming!"

I looked at him and he looked at me, then we both jumped off our swings and grabbed our canteens and ran for the back door. I beat Buck by a mile 'cause he tripped on his canteen strap.

Mom wasn't in the kitchen so I looked in the living room but she wasn't there, either. "Mom!" I yelled. "We want to go swimming!" I listened but I didn't hear her anywhere. "Mom!" I yelled again as Bucky came in, picking grass off his knees.

"What?!"

I jumped and turned around and Mom was standing in the basement door with a big basket of laundry. She wiped her forehead and looked at both of us and our canteens.

"Can we go swimming?"

"If you can find somebody to take you," she said, going past with the basket so we had to back out of the way. On the way upstairs she said, "Your dad has the car and I've got too much work to do."

Buck said, "We can call my house."

"Okay," I said, listening to Mom walking around in Megan's room. I heard the basket drop on the floor, then Mom yelled like she does when she hurts herself.

"You okay, Mom?" I yelled up the stairs.

"Yes, now go outside! I'm trying to clean!" Buck dialed and let the phone ring twenty times but his mom didn't answer. He called back in case he got the wrong number and let it ring and ring, then Mom came downstairs with a load of dirty laundry and kicked us outside again.

*   *   *

"How far is it to the pool if we walked?" Buck said, taking another drink from his canteen and putting his feet up on the side of the tree house.

"Too far," I said. "Besides, I don't know how to get there." I put my feet up too, then wiggled my toes when a fly landed on them.

"I think I do," Buck said, taking another drink. "Isn't the gas station where they grow the corn on the way?"

"Yeah, I think so," I said. I knew the gas station he was talking about. They grow a couple rows of corn out front every year. "Why do you think they grow that corn?"

"To eat it."

"Yeah, but don't you think people sneak up and take it when it's ready?"

"Maybe they watch it when it gets close. I would."

"Oh," I said, trying to think of something else we could do that was as good as sneaking some corn.

Buck got up and looked at the ground, then out at the big branch goin' back to the swing set. He leaned out a little and put his arms around the branch but they barely went halfway down the sides. He leaned his head over and looked down again. "You ever look into that hole down there to see if the tree's rotten?"

"Nope," I said. "Squirrels go in there. You get bit on the face by a squirrel and you have to get rabies shots in your head."

Buck climbed over the edge of the tree house and

scooted out on the branch, his legs wrapped around it real tight. "Where you goin'?" I said, sitting up.

"I don't know," Buck said, scooting out a little more and looking down again. He bent over and rested his whole body on the branch, his chin touching right where the branch went out flat across the yard.

I stood and pointed where the tire swing was tied to the tree. "Crawl out and climb down the rope," I said. "I've done that lots of times."

Buck sat up and turned back. "You ever climb up the rope and get on the branch?"

"I tried but I can't grab anything to pull my legs up. Dad can do it."

Buck sat there a while, looking out at the rope. He looked back at his canteen but I could see him decide not to get off the branch to get it. Across the alley the air conditioning went off in the big brick house.

"Wish we had an air conditioner," Bucky said.

"Me too," I said. "Mom wants one real bad but Dad says they cost too much."

Buck scooted out on the branch till he was at the top of the bend, then sat up real slow. "I bet I could make it all the way to the end," he said.

"Bet'cha can't," I said. "You'll chicken out or fall off."

"How do you know? You never done it."

"Mom and Dad had a party last year and that's what happened to a college kid. He chickened out half-way and they had to get the ladder for him, then he fell off the ladder."

"He get hurt?"

"It killed him," I said, trying not to laugh when

Buck turned around and looked at me all big-eyed.

"You're lyin'," Buck said putting his hands on the branch and looking out again.

"He broke his legs is all."

"No he didn't."

"Okay, he fell off the ladder and landed on another guy, and the ladder fell on both of 'em. They got a couple cuts."

"Big deal," Buck said. "I've been hurt worse than that." He scooted out a little more, looking at the thick rope wrapped twice around the branch.

"How you gonna get over that?" I said.

Buck stared at the rope. It made the branch so thick you couldn't spread your legs wide and crawl across it. Instead, you had to sit up and climb over. The first time I got past it I felt pretty good until I realized I had to turn all the way around to get back. It scared me 'cause nobody was home, but that was good too 'cause I woulda got in a lot of trouble.

"I don't know," Bucky said, scooting out a little more. He tried reaching out real slow to see if he could touch the rope but it was still too far away. "Maybe I can kinda hop over it."

Right then I got a sick feeling he might do something dumb and fall off, and I thought about going in and telling Mom. "Don't go too fast," I said. "Are your hands sweaty?"

"No," Bucky said. "But I sure am thirsty."

I took a drink from my canteen, then got his and tried to hand it to him, but I had to lean on the branch and swing it out by the strap. He caught it first try, but then he tried to drink with one hand while he was holding the branch with the other and he dropped it. The canteen landed on the edge of the bare dirt under the tire swing and the water ran out, making a little muddy lake.

"Let me have yours," Buck said.

"Forget it. You'll drop it."

"I'm thirsty."

"So?"

"So gimme a drink."

"Go out and touch the rope first."

"Why?"

"'Cause that's what you gotta do to get a drink."

Buck sat a minute, then scooted out a bit, leaned over and reached his hand way out, but he still wasn't far enough. "You sure this old tree ain't rotten? What if it's got Dutch elm disease? This whole branch could fall off."

"Dad says it's okay."

Buck pushed himself back up and sat still again, then scooted out real slow, holding on like he thought a tornado was gonna come along and blow him out of the tree. I took another long drink from my canteen because watching him was making my mouth dry.

Bucky scooted out a bit more without reaching for the rope. He did it again and again, then all of a sudden he could touch the rope easy, almost without bending over. When he turned to look back at me he did it so slow I thought maybe he had a bee on his face, but he was smiling as big as I'd ever seen him.

"I made it," he said.

"Bucky, what are you doing!" I turned around and I could make out Mom's face behind an upstairs screen. "Don't move, Bucky! You stay right there!"

"You're in for it now, Buck," I said. He looked back at me and started to turn around, but then his hand slipped on the bark and he hugged the branch like he was holding on to a rocket that was going to the moon.

Mom came out the back door and ran out to the tire, looking up at Buck. He looked down at her, smiling a little. "I'm okay," he said.

Mom said, "What are you doing out there?"

Bucky sat up but Mom got all white and made like she was gonna catch him. That scared Buck so much he laid down again and grabbed the branch. "I had to touch the rope to get a drink of water," he said.

Mom turned and looked at me holding my canteen. I didn't know what to say to get out of it so I didn't say anything. "You made Bucky go out there for a drink of water?"

"I didn't make him go out there," I said. "He was already out there."

Mom looked back at Buck and he smiled again, and I could tell she wasn't going to get it figured out. But that was good too, because I was pretty sure I could get him in as much trouble as I was in if I had enough time to think about it.

"I'm going to get a ladder, okay, Bucky? You just wait right there, okay?"

"Okay," he said, like all of a sudden he was having fun.

"You want some help, Mom? The ladder's pretty heavy."

"You get down here and be quiet," she said, heading for the garage.

Buck sat up again and turned toward me. "It's not so bad out here once you get used to it."

"Oh yeah?" I said. "Wait till you're on the ground and she's not worried you're gonna fall anymore." I climbed down and I could hear Mom trying to open the squeaky old garage doors.

"You think she'll tell my mom?" Bucky whispered, looking down at me.

"I don't know," I said. "Slide down the rope before she gets back with the ladder."

Bucky looked at the rope like he was thinking about it.

"C'mon," I said. "Get down before she comes back and we can hide."

"What if I fall?"

"You aren't gonna fall," I said, trying not to think about it. "Just get your legs around the rope and you'll be okay."

Bucky leaned out a little and looked down the side of the branch at the rope. He felt down with one hand, trying to reach the knot, but you can't feel it 'cause it's right under the branch. "You gotta start down first before you can grab the rope," I said.

"What?" Bucky said, like I just told him a two-foot spider was on his leg. "Where's your mom?"

"Hurry up you wiener," I said, quiet like, 'cause I could hear Mom in the garage, trying to get the ladder down from the rafters. "Just swing your legs down."

Bucky turned a little to the side and hung one leg down, trying to feel the rope. He missed it about ten times before his toe hit it, then he kicked it again a couple times to be sure. "That it?" he asked.

"Yeah. Now slide down until you can get your feet around it."

Bucky slid down a little more and hooked his heel around the rope, then he let his other leg down until he was lying half sideways across the branch. He felt around with his hands until he had good holds on the bark, then he scooted down even more and got the rope between both feet. "I got it," he said.

I heard some banging and looked at the garage, then I heard Mom swear. It sounded like she was trying to get the ladder loose from the screens it always gets stuck on. "Hurry up," I said, running around Bucky's side of the tree so Mom couldn't see me.

Bucky scooted down more, then I saw him try to reach back up. "I'm stuck," he said, sounding scared.

"Keep going," I said, peeking around the tree.

"I can't get back up," he said, his voice all squeaky.

"I told you, you can't climb up. You can only climb down. Come on, she's coming!"

Bucky moved down a little more and got the rope good between his shins. He had one arm up around the branch and brought the other one down, feeling for the rope. "Where is it?"

"Over more." He missed it. "More." He missed it again. "Come on, Buck! Slide down more."

Buck slid down a bit more, then all of a sudden he came off the branch. I thought he was gonna fall right on me, but instead he reached out and grabbed the rope in front of him and hung on it like a monkey. He looked down and I couldn't remember seeing his eyes as big as they were. "Tell your Mom to hurry," he said.

"What for?" I said, leaning around the tree trunk to look at the garage. "You got the rope." I could see the ladder backing out of the garage, then going back in again. I looked up at Buck and he was looking at the rope, then at the branch above him, like he was trying to figure out what happened. "Come on," I whispered.

I could see the ladder coming into the backyard and Mom yelled, "Hang on Bucky, I'm coming!"

Right then Bucky slid down the rope, landed on the tire and bounced onto me. "Ow," he said. "I burned my hands."

"Ssshhh," I said, grabbing him. The front end of the ladder was coming around one side of the tree, so I pulled Bucky around the other side until we could see the back end. A moment later the ladder stopped, then it started slowly swinging around.

Bucky was looking at his palms and I could tell they hurt. Mom said, "All right you guys. Not funny!" and I almost laughed. I looked at Bucky and he had to bite his lip to keep from laughing too.

The ladder swung away and disappeared, and for a minute I thought Mom might be coming around the tree. Then the other end appeared and I could see she was headed back to the garage. We moved around the trunk and stayed quiet until I could hear her putting the ladder away.

"She's gone," I said, peeking around the tree at the garage.

"I did it, " Buck said, squeezing his hands closed, then opening them again. "I thought sure I was gonna fall."

"I thought you were too," I said.

"If my mom saw me do that she wouldn't let me come over here for a year."

"Yeah," I said. "Or maybe ever."

"Yeah," Buck said, looking up at the rope. "I bet we could climb back up," he said.

From the back of the house Mom called out. "I want to see you boys when it gets dark, and not a minute before." I listened for the back door slamming but I didn't hear it. "Answer me!" she said.

"Okay!" we both said, staying hidden.

Mom said something else but I didn't figure it out until I heard the back door slam shut. Bucky picked up his canteen and drank the water that was left, then climbed on the tire and swung back and forth, holding the rope with his arms 'cause his hands still hurt. I climbed on the tire on the other side. "School starts next week," I said.

"Yeah, I know," Buck said, leaning back and looking up at the branch. "I'm gonna tell everybody."

I looked up at the branch too, and we stayed on the tire, letting it swing back and forth until it was almost still. I thought about telling Bucky I'd never climbed down the rope, and Bucky just kept smiling.

SCHOOL

~ *September* ~

Mom dropped me at Bucky's so we could walk to school together, but before I even got up on his porch it started raining again. I rang the bell and pulled my plastic poncho out of the lid of my lunchbox. While I was putting it on Bucky came out wearing his yellow raincoat that weighs about fifty pounds. He looked so hot under the hood that he was already red in the face.

Bucky yelled, "I'm goin'!", then slammed the door behind him real hard.

"What's the matter?" I said, looking at my pudding and wishing I could eat it right then and at lunch too.

"I hate my mom," Bucky said, dropping down the steps.

He was halfway across his backyard before I got my lunchbox closed and caught up with him. "Why?" I said, thinking he was more red in the face from being mad than being hot.

"Because she hates *me*," he said, smacking his new lunchbox against a tree trunk. He checked it to see if he dented it.

We went through the hedge into the alley, then Buck glanced back to make sure his mom couldn't see him if she was looking out. He undid the top buckles on his raincoat and pulled his hood back, letting the rain mess up his new haircut. I kept my hood up 'cause the rain was cold.

We cut across a corner of the alley and onto the field. I looked at the school up on the hill, then felt my pocket for my homework and it was still there. We'd been assigned to write a page with two people having a conversation about anything we wanted. "You get your story done for Mrs. Blaske?" I asked.

"Yeah," Buck said. "Last night I still couldn't think what two people would talk about so I yelled down to Mom to see if she'd help. She yelled back, 'I don't have time!'" He said it real high like his mom talks when she's makin' a big deal out of something. "So I just wrote that down. Then I wrote down me sayin' 'Why not?' and her yelling back more, until I had a whole page of it." Bucky slicked his hair back and pulled his hood up, leaving it open.

"I got a great idea last night watchin' Mom talk on the phone," I said. "I could tell what she was talking about and what the girl on the phone was asking her by what Mom said, so I wrote the whole page like that. Like a phone call, where you can only hear one person."

Bucky looked at me a couple times, then said, "How come I never think of things like that?"

We were at the bottom of the hill when the outside bell rang. We ran up the hill but it was so slick we kept falling down. By the time we got to the door we were late and had mud all over our pants and shoes.

We went in and up the stairs to the third floor and hung our coats on our hooks. I scraped my shoes off on each other before going into Mrs. Blaske's class. Bucky went to his desk and I went to mine on the other side of the room. When I took my seat Mrs. Blaske gave me a dirty look but didn't say anything 'cause the school nurse was talking to the class.

The nurse said, "Don't forget to bring this form back by Friday. If you've already had a TB tine test we need your doctor to sign the card. The rest of you will be getting the test next Friday. Not this coming Friday, but the next one."

The nurse looked at Mrs. Blaske and Mrs. Blaske smiled. "I'll remind them," she said. The nurse left and Mrs. Blaske went up front where she always stands. "Pass your assignments up," she said.

I dug my paper out of my pocket and unfolded it, then passed it up with the ones behind me. Mrs. Blaske collected them and put them in a pile. I scraped my shoes on the legs of my desk, trying to get the rest of the mud off.

Mrs. Blaske dug around in a desk drawer for a minute and said, "Does anyone remember the name of the woman who studies the monkeys we were reading about?" I raised my hand and so did Cindy Ree and a couple other kids.

Mrs. Blaske looked up. "Cindy?"

"Jane Goodheart," Cindy said, and I wondered again how she could sit up straight like she did all day, without slouching or resting her head on her desk. I couldn't sit up more than a couple minutes without getting sore.

"That's close," Mrs. Blaske said. My arm was getting tired so I propped it up with my other hand. Mrs. Blaske called on one of the other kids, but he got it wrong too. I looked out the window and it was still raining, the water running in streaks down the windows. I figured we'd get stuck inside again for recess, which was okay as long as we got to play dodgeball.

Mrs. Blaske turned around to get a book off her desk and Mike Craig shot me in the cheek with a spitball. I pulled it off my face and flicked it back at him but it landed on Mary Olden's desk and she squealed.

Mrs. Blaske got a Kleenex out of her drawer and handed it to me and I went over and picked up the spitball and put it in the trash. I sat down and Mrs. Blaske stared at me from right beside my desk. "You'll stay after school five minutes and think about the way you've been behaving lately," she said. Mike Craig giggled. "You too, Mike," she said, and he stopped.

She looked around the room to see if there was anyone else she wanted to keep after school, and while she was doing that I could see a big white hair that was growing up inside her nose. Bucky spotted it the first day of school but I didn't believe him until right then.

"Her first name is Jane," Mrs. Blaske said, walking back up to her spot. "What was her last name?" She turned around and I was the only one with my hand up. I looked over at Bucky 'cause I knew he knew the answer, but he was staring out the window by his desk at the rain and gray clouds. Mrs. Blaske looked around the room, waiting, and Cindy raised her hand again.

Mrs. Blaske pointed at Cindy like she was happy not to have to call on me.

"May I please be excused, Mrs. Blaske?"

Mrs. Blaske twitched her lips real tight and nodded. I put my hand down, and when she turned to me I made sure I was looking out the door at Cindy walking down the hall. "Her name is Jane Goodall," Mrs. Blaske said. "She was born in London, England, in nineteen thirty-four."

*   *   *

It was our class's turn to go to the library, so when Mrs. Blaske let us out I ran down the stairs and down the hall. Then I had to go all the way back up to the room and do it again without running, so I was last in line at the library door.

In the library I looked for my favorite space book but it still wasn't back on the shelf. I went over to Mrs. Nancy's desk to tell her it wasn't back like she said it would be, but when I got there I had to wait in another line. I didn't mind though because Mrs. Nancy always has books I like and knows right where they are.

When it was my turn I said, "I can't find the space book."

Mrs. Nancy reached down under a table by her desk and pulled up the space book. She smiled and handed it to me, then gave me another book. On the cover were two big boys and a girl looking around in a cave.

"We're going to make a deal," Mrs. Nancy said. "You can check out *Rockets and Space* again, but you have to take this one too, and read it. There's a whole series if you like it."

I looked at the book like it smelled bad. "I can't even read the title," I said.

"Yes you can. Go on."

I looked at it again, then I said, "*Student Sle... Sleeah....*"

"*Sleuths.*"

"*Sleuths...*" I said, sounding like I knew what it meant, and hoping Mrs. Nancy wouldn't ask me. "*...in The Secret of Treasure Cave.*" I looked inside the cover and there was a picture showing the sleuth kids in a spooky house, with a creepy shadow coming from a door they were looking at. "What's the secret?" I said.

"You'll have to read it and see," she said.

I flipped through the pages and it was pretty long, but I wanted the space book so I took it. Mrs. Nancy helped me check them both out and gave me two bookmarks. I looked around for Bucky but everyone was gone already so I went back up to class. I was the last one in my chair and when I sat down Mrs. Blaske said, "Take out a pencil and a piece of paper. We're going to have a spelling quiz."

Everybody groaned and got out their papers and pencils, and right then the wind picked up, throwing more rain on the windows. I watched the rain run down the glass, then looked over at Bucky. He looked back, then put his head down on his desk by his paper and got his pencil ready.

*　　*　　*

Mrs. Blaske took another paper off her desk and graded it. I was tired of looking at the space book so I put it back in my desk and got out the sleuth book.

Cindy Ree was reading a couple rows over, still sitting up straight as a post. Mike Craig had his desk in a corner for throwing more spitballs. The rest of the class was pretending to read while they messed around and wrote notes, but I knew Mrs. Blaske was watching me so I didn't fool around. I looked at the pictures in the sleuth book, then I looked up at the clock and it still wasn't time to go to lunch. There wasn't anything else to do, so I started reading.

On the first page it said:

STUDENT SLEUTHS WANTED!

Brave hearts needed! Mysteries await!
All students urged to apply!
(Even if you don't like school!)

I didn't like school so right there I knew why Mrs. Nancy gave me the book. A little lower down on the page I saw one of the boy's names was Coyote Cal, and that didn't sound like the name of someone who liked school either.

"All right," Mrs. Blaske said, and when I looked up she was standing on her spot again, holding the graded papers. "Clear your desks."

I put my book away and Mrs. Blaske walked around the room, handing back the conversation papers we'd written. I was excited 'cause I didn't usually do good on papers, but I knew this one was different. I could feel it.

Mrs. Blaske went by a few times. "Your papers were very good," she said. "I was surprised. Some of you show a very definite imagination."

Mrs. Blaske dropped my paper on my desk. It had a big red *X* on it, and across the top, in red pen, she had written: *This doesn't make any sense.*

I looked at the paper a long time, not seeing the places where she fixed my spelling and punctuation, but just staring at the big red *X*. I looked around and most of the kids by me had check marks or plusses, and Cindy Ree had a gold star.

Mrs. Blaske stopped again on her spot. "I want you to copy your papers over now, and fix the errors I've noted. You may change anything you don't like, but those changes will be graded for errors as well." She went back and sat down at her desk and started checking the spelling quizzes.

I sat there, feeling rotten, until I realized Mrs. Blaske didn't get that it was a phone call. She thought it was just one person talking to himself. When I looked up Maggie Long was at Mrs. Blaske's desk with her paper, so I went up with mine.

When Maggie went back to her desk I held out my paper and said, "This is a phone call. Between two people. They're talkin' but you only get to hear one of them." Mrs. Blaske took the paper and looked at it. "You can tell what the other person is saying by what that person says."

Mrs. Blaske handed the paper back. "It's not what I assigned," she said. "You were to write a conversation between two people."

"But that is two people," I said. "It's one person you can read and the other person they're talking to."

"It doesn't make any sense," Mrs. Blaske said. "Go sit down."

I looked at the paper and it made sense to me. I looked at Mrs. Blaske again, tryin' to figure out why she couldn't see it and I could. "Go sit down," she said again, but I didn't move. I looked at the paper, trying to think why she couldn't see it.

The lunch bell rang and Mrs. Blaske stood up. "No running," she said as the kids all ran out the door. I looked at Mrs. Blaske, then I crumpled up the paper and threw it in the trash basket by her desk. I walked out without looking at her again but I could tell she was looking at me.

*   *   *

In the gym I got my school milk and took my lunchbox over to the end of a table where Bucky was sitting. He'd already eaten everything in his box except for a plastic bag full of green seaweed crackers that his mom packed. "I saw the hair in Mrs. Blaske's nose," I said, taking a big bite of my peanut butter and jelly sandwich. It had grape jelly, which I hated.

Bucky pushed one of the seaweed crackers to the edge of the table, then nudged it onto the floor. "I told you," he said.

"I hate her. She gave me an *X* for my paper. She didn't even get it is how stupid she is." I took another big bite of my sandwich, then shoved some corn chips in my mouth.

"She ain't stupider than my mom," Bucky said, pushing another seaweed cracker off the table. "My mom's the stupidest person that ever lived."

"How come?" I said through the glob of chips in my mouth. I tried to open my milk but it was one of those you get every once in a while that won't open right.

Bucky pushed another cracker onto the floor, then picked up his foot and smashed the crackers flat. When he lifted his shoe all that was left was a little green dust on the gym floor. He looked at the bottom of his shoe and laughed, then showed me the crackers all jammed up in the treads and I laughed too.

I got the milk carton open by ripping it and spilling milk on myself. I took a big drink and my mouth started working again.

Bucky said, "She says I can't have Christmas at Dad's this year. I gotta stay here."

"How come?" I said, taking a bite of my sandwich so big I could hardly chew.

"She says it's her turn."

I took another big swig of milk and choked the sandwich down. "I thought you were here last year," I said, looking over at Megan when her first-grade class walked in the door.

Bucky leaned way back, keeping himself from falling over by putting his feet against the bottom of the table. "She says last year doesn't count because it was supposed to be his turn and he didn't take me."

"That's stupid," I said, finishing my sandwich and opening my pudding. I put a spoonful in my mouth and squished it back and forth through my front teeth.

"I told you," Bucky said.

*　　*　　*

Mrs. Blaske held up the quizzes and said, "I am going to hand these back, then we'll go over the answers." I watched her as she moved around the room, handing the tests back, but when she came down my row I stared at the floor. I was gonna go the whole rest of the week without looking at her once.

A minute later she came up from the back of the class and dropped my quiz on my desk. It had a big plus on it, and out of all ten words I only spelled *character* wrong because I used an *o* instead of an *e*.

"All right," Mrs. Blaske said from her spot. "Raise your hand if you got them all correct."

I looked over at Cindy to see her put her hand up but she didn't. I leaned over a bit and looked at her paper and I could see she'd gotten three wrong. I felt pretty good about that and didn't see anybody with their hand up until I turned the other way. Nat Stone was holding his hand up and smiling. I almost yelled out that he cheated but I couldn't prove it, even though everybody knows Nat Stone cheats at everything.

Mrs. Blaske said, "If you think you got it right and I marked it wrong, come up after we're done going over the words. I went through these pretty fast and sometimes I can't tell your writing."

She went down the list, reading the right spelling for each word. I looked over at Nat and he wasn't paying any attention to his paper. I looked at *charactor* on my list, then I looked at it real close because it almost looked like the *o* was an *e*, but it wasn't.

I looked at Nat again and he was smiling. I slipped a pencil out of my desk, then I had to get another one 'cause the first one didn't have an eraser. I hunched over real low like I was following along with the words Mrs. Blaske was reading, then I snuck the pencil up and erased the *o* in *charactor* and replaced it with an *e*.

I looked at it and it looked pretty good, but you could still see some of the *o* smudged on the paper, so I erased it until I could only see clean paper underneath. When Mrs. Blaske turned around for a minute I put the pencil away.

"Did anyone have any right that I marked wrong?" she said, turning back. Warren Mills and Sissy Gant both raised their hands. I got all hot thinking about lying, but I put my hand up too, real low.

"All right, you three come on up. The rest of you copy the words you missed on the back of your paper three times each." The way Mike Craig groaned I figured he missed them all.

I waited until Warren and Sissy got to Mrs. Blaske's desk, then I walked up and stood behind them. Mrs. Blaske looked at Sissy's paper, fixed her score, and Sissy sat down. When she looked at Warren's paper she said if he thought his *f* was an *f* he was wrong, and that it looked like a *t*. Warren sat down and slammed the lid on his desk.

Mrs. Blaske looked right into me as I gave her my paper. She looked at it and held it up a little, then looked back at me. "Did you erase this?" she asked.

I got kinda sick right then and I wished I wasn't

up there at all. I remembered my dad sayin' liars end up in jail or rich and all of a sudden I didn't want to take a chance like that. "Yeah," I said, thinking about how somebody would be calling my mom again from the principal's office.

"All right," Mrs. Blaske said. Then she changed the grade from nine to ten, put a *Super* at the top and handed me the paper. I looked at it and looked at her and I didn't get it at all. Even when I took the paper and sat down and didn't hear anything anybody said for the next ten minutes I didn't get what happened at all.

The only thing I heard before the bell rang was Nat leaning over to me and saying, "You cheated."

* * *

Bucky waited in the hall while me and Mike sat out our five minutes and promised not to get in any more trouble. I read some of the *Student Sleuths* book and it was a lot better than I thought it would be. The sleuths were going to a place called Typhoon Island, where they were going to investigate old stories about pirate treasure.

When Mrs. Blaske let us go I took the sleuths book and left the space book in my desk. It wasn't raining hard anymore but the field was soaked so Bucky and I went along the alley instead of cutting across the field.

I told him what happened because he's the best person I know at figuring things out. Once he even figured out his mom had candy hidden in the house because she brushed her teeth in the middle of the day. I didn't believe him at first, but after she went out we found a whole bag of toffee.

"I still don't get it," I said, looking down through the neck of my poncho at the spelling list.

Bucky said, "She asked if you erased it because she was sure you were gonna lie about it."

"Why'd she give me the point for it then?"

"'Cause she thought you were sayin' you erased it when you wrote it. You wouldn't say you changed it if you were cheating."

"What?" I said.

"You wouldn't change it and then say you erased it if you were tryin' to cheat. You'd say you didn't erase it, but then she'd know you were lying 'cause you can see it's been changed." We stopped and Bucky stuck his hand in the neck of my poncho, pointing at the paper. "You can see right there. The paper's all rough and you can tell somebody erased something."

I thought about it hard and I could almost see what he was sayin'. "She thought I was gonna lie."

"Yeah," Bucky said, getting quieter the closer we got to his house. He kicked some gravel down the alley, then stomped right through a puddle in his shoes.

"I don't like her thinkin' I'm a liar," I said.

We climbed up through the bushes in his backyard and walked across the lawn. Bucky had his head down and kept kicking the grass. He looked out at the street when we got to the front porch and said, "Oh, great."

I looked where he was looking and his mom's car was sitting at the curb where it always was. She didn't usually come home until later, and all of a sudden I didn't want to go in and play with Bucky anymore. "I better get home," I said. "You want to come over?"

Bucky kicked the bottom step. "Can't," he said.

I pulled out the *Student Sleuths* book and showed it to him. "Mrs. Nancy gave me this. She said there's a bunch more just like it."

Bucky looked at the cover, then inside at some of the pictures, then handed it back. "I gotta go," he said, climbing the porch steps and kicking each one on the way up.

"Okay," I said. "See you tomorrow."

"Yeah," Bucky said, then he opened the front door and went in. He slammed the door and I could hear him stomping up the steps to his room.

I put the book back under my poncho and went up the sidewalk, thinking about Mrs. Blaske being so sure I was a liar. I got mad about it but it wore off some before I got home. It wasn't raining at all under the big elm trees on Summit Street, and the sun came out a few times but I couldn't find a rainbow.

I sat on the front porch and thought about telling Mom and Dad what happened, but I didn't want to tell them the part about cheating so I decided to forget it. It made me mad that Mrs. Blaske thought I wouldn't tell the truth, and then when I did tell the truth she didn't hear it. I thought about robbing a bank, and the police catching me and telling me I had to confess, only when I did they gave me all the money and told me I could keep it.

For a minute I thought Mrs. Blaske thought she was pretty smart, then I remembered her not getting my paper and giving me a big red *X* and I hated her for that too. It made me mad that I'd thrown the paper away 'cause I thought it was a good paper no matter what she said. I thought about going back to school to get it but then I remembered the janitor coming in and emptying the trash while I was sitting at my desk after class.

I pulled the quiz out and looked at it again and thought about Mom and Dad seeing I got them all right and maybe giving me some ice cream for it. Then I remembered the look on Nat Stone's face. I hated Nat and I didn't want to be like him, or like Mrs. Blaske.

I crumpled up the quiz and went around the side of the house. The lid was off on one of the garbage cans and the bottom was full of rain water. A paper trash bag was falling apart in the water and moldy orange peels were floating out the side. I threw the quiz in the water and watched it sink.

THE PATCH

~ October ~

It was the weekend before Halloween and it was windy and cold, but I didn't notice it much 'cause we were running so hard. We were running because we had to stay and help Dad with the screens and storm windows longer than I thought, so we were late getting down to the tracks.

Bucky and I took the alley most of the way so no one would see us, but when we got to the tracks he said he dropped his ski mask so we had to go back and look for it. "Hurry up and find it!" I yelled, because I could see how low the sun was getting. It looked like it would be dark by the time we got back and I didn't like the idea of being down on the tracks after dark.

"I got it!" Bucky yelled, pulling it out of the weeds between the ruts in the alley. He put it on like a cap, leaving the mask part with the eye holes pushed up on his head.

We slid down the hill into the tall dry weeds along the tracks. Bucky yanked on a pine branch to keep from going too fast and I slid into it, getting sap on my face. "Sorry," he said, not stopping to see if I got my eye poked out or anything.

I scraped the sap off best as I could and tried to stick it on Bucky, but he took off running through the weeds. I went after him, but by the time I caught up we were standing on the tracks, and it was so spooky down there I forgot about getting him back. We might have decided not to go at all if we hadn't been chasing each other, but before we thought about it we were standing on the rails, looking up and down the tracks for anything worth seeing.

Even with the sun still up it was getting dark in the ravine the tracks ran through. A block away the top of the Summit Street bridge was still in the sun, but the bottom was all dark in shadow. It looked scary like that, and I was glad we weren't going that way because I didn't want to walk under all that creaky wood.

I grabbed Bucky and yelled "Boo!" but he didn't even jump, so I started balancing my way down a rail to the yard. Bucky caught up beside me on the other rail, but he kept falling off more than he was on. I pretended not to be watching the tall weeds along the ditch as much as I was, but they were so big a werewolf could hide in them easy, which was what I was worried was in there.

"You could hide a werewolf in those weeds, Buck," I said. "A big one."

"There aren't any werewolves in Iowa. Never have been."

"How do you know? A werewolf coulda come right along this track a million years ago. And don't say there weren't any train tracks a million years ago."

"There weren't any tracks a million years ago."

"I know there weren't. But you can't know about a werewolf."

Bucky fell off the rail and stayed off. "I know there haven't ever been any werewolves here," he said. "And even if there has there aren't any in those weeds." Bucky knows a lot so it made me feel better, but I reminded myself to think of something he didn't know so we'd be even.

When we got close to the rail yard the sun fell behind a row of old boxcars sitting on one of the sidings. I stopped balancing on the rails and looked for spikes that had popped out of the ties, but I didn't find any. We passed the switch that connected the two main tracks running back up around the curve, but it was locked so we couldn't throw it. Up the side of the ravine we passed the end of Lucas Street just as the street-light came on, but the light only made everything seem darker down in the yard.

We climbed up the short ladder on a flatcar in the middle of the boxcars, then walked the length of the car on beat-up old wooden planks before climbing down the other side. Like we always did we talked about what we'd do if the train started moving, but I knew the train wasn't going to move. You can hear the engines up and down the yard when they're working, and the only sound I heard was a car driving by that I couldn't see.

We kicked gravel into the puddles in the ditch as we walked along the far side of the yard. The frogs got quiet when we went by, but hummed real loud ahead and behind us. A couple minutes later we got quiet ourselves because we were getting close. Bucky pulled his mask down over his face, and I got mine out and pulled it on. It was scratchy but it made me feel safe.

On the other side of an empty siding, up the far side of the ravine, was an open field that used to have corrals for loading cattle before they took them out. Since then the people who lived in the houses across the street used the old pasture for their gardens, and Buck and I got used to picking things there on our trips to the yard. I looked down the siding at a tanker car sitting in front of the sunset. "Don't get anything bigger than you can carry," I said.

"How big is that?" Bucky said, hunching down.

"Well we might have to run or something so you don't want one so big you can't."

"Oh," Buck said, like he does when he's thinking. "Maybe we should go back and get a wagon."

That was something I hadn't thought of. Seeing how scary the yard was getting I thought it was a good idea, because if we went all the way home I knew we'd decide not to come back.

"Nah, it's too far," Bucky said, jumping the ditch and disappearing into the weeds. I thought about slugging him when I caught up, but I was glad he was going first up the side of the ravine. I used to always go first because I was afraid of getting jumped from behind, but then one night with Bucky and the Figgin brothers I ran up on a coon that almost bit my foot.

When we got up to the edge of the old pasture we stayed low, looking across the rows of vegetables in the different gardens. Frost had killed some of the plants, but others were still standing. "Where's the patch?" Buck said, all whispery.

I pointed at the end of the field toward the sunset.

"On the other side of that corn," I said, looking at four long rows of dry stalks running from our side of the gardens to the side by the street. We crouched and moved along the edge of the old pasture until we got to the end of the corn rows, then we stopped, looking around. "If we go in through the corn nobody'll see us," I said.

Bucky nodded, looking around at everything like he was waiting for a reason to jump. "You go first," he said.

I thought about arguing but it was getting dark fast and I could feel the cold coming through my jacket. Staying low I crawled past a few rows of rotted greens, then along an empty row of holes that looked like they used to be beets, and the whole time Bucky kept running up against my feet until I kicked him. We waited a second, listening to the thousand little nothings you hear when it's quiet and you're being sneaky, then I squeezed in under the big bottom leaves of the corn plants with Bucky right behind.

There were so many leaves over our heads I was sure no one would see us even if they were standing right next to the stalks. As I crawled I slipped over two rows until we were one row away from the patch. When I stopped Bucky crawled up beside me. It wasn't the biggest I'd ever seen, but most of the vines had dried up so I knew the pumpkins were ripe and would pull off easy. I saw a gourd a foot away and pointed at it, but when Bucky reached for it I smacked him.

"What?" he said, a little high-pitched.

"You don't know where the vine goes. You pull, as dry as it is, it might make the whole patch rattle."

"Oh," he said, kind of big-eyed about the idea of that much noise.

I looked around the patch, trying to see the best way in, then I looked at the houses across the street. Most of them had lights on inside but there wasn't anybody moving around outside. I pushed between two corn plants and they rustled a bit.

Bucky grabbed me. "Where you goin?" he said, even more squeaky.

"Where do you think I'm goin'?"

Bucky looked at the patch, then back at me. He didn't look scared exactly, but he wasn't happy about leaving the corn plants. I wiggled between the stalks again and Bucky grabbed me again. "I wish I had my slingshot," he said.

"It's busted."

"I know. I wish I had it anyway."

And there I was, not wanting to go out through the corn because I wished we had his slingshot too, busted or not. Bucky's always doing that to me, getting me thinking about things that wouldn't have popped into my head by themselves. Sometimes it's good like when he said maybe it was an electrified sheep fence and it turned out it was, but most of the time it just gets me thinking too much.

"What'cha waitin' for?" he said.

I turned and looked at Buck, who was looking at me like he didn't know what I could be waiting for after he stopped me twice from going. I couldn't think how to answer so I pulled his mask down, gave him a punch and squeezed out of the corn before he hit me back.

I didn't like it out under the open sky, but it was

already so dark I knew it'd be hard to see us. I crawled along an open row between the patch and the corn, looking for the best way in so I didn't have to stand up and look around like some stupid gopher.

I felt Bucky on my heels again but this time I was glad he was close. If anybody came up behind us they'd get him first and I might have a chance to get away. Then I thought about coons again, and about running into one face first, but I decided it was better gettin' bit than gettin' caught, unless the coon had rabies.

When I found a break in the patch I nosed in. The little opening led into a small clearing with a few paths leading farther into the tangle of vines. I wiggled in and stayed low, then waited until Bucky crawled up beside me.

"You sure took your time about it," he said, kinda winded.

"We're here ain't we?" I said, like I knew what I'd been doing all along. I noticed a round shadow and slid my hand out. I rapped it and it made a hollow thump.

"What was that!" Bucky whispered, grabbing me.

I pointed at the big pumpkin sitting there covered by a couple dried-up vines. Bucky touched it, then gave it a thump himself. It sounded great.

"It seems kinda small," said Buck. "But maybe we should take it."

"Let's keep looking," I said. "No sense not getting good ones as long as we're here."

I moved on before Bucky said something I didn't want to hear, like I knew he would. Keeping my eyes low I could see where to go against the last light in the sky, and after we moved another ten feet we found ourselves surrounded by a ring of pumpkins. There were all different kinds, some tall like jelly beans and others squat and round like giant apples, and a big one that leaned on my shoulder when I scooted over so Bucky could crawl up beside me again.

I looked at Bucky and I could make out a big grin through his mask. We got the giggles a bit and tried to keep quiet but it was great being alone in that patch with all those pumpkins. Then, right when I was trying hard not to laugh out loud, I got the kind of chill that goes all the way down to your feet and feels like someone jabbed an icicle in the back of your neck.

I reached out to grab Bucky but he got me first so I knew he'd heard it too. It was quiet again for a minute, then Bucky jumped and I knew he'd heard it again like me. He squirmed and I had to grab him to keep him from running off. It was a tinkling chain, and when we heard it again it was getting closer.

"It's a –!"

I shoved my hand over Bucky's mouth and partway in. He bit me back, but he shut up, and that was all I cared about. I wasn't worried a person would hear us, but dogs have ears that hear things nobody else can hear. I think Bucky remembered too, 'cause he got real still as the jangling chain came closer.

I got so scared listening to the chain getting louder and louder that I felt like I weighed a ton but could jump to the moon at the same time. I kept a hold of Bucky because I was sure he would try to run for it if I let go, like you could outrun a dog in the dark.

We heard someone whistle, and that was better and worse. It was better because it meant it wasn't a stray, 'cause they can be pretty mean if they haven't eaten in a while. I'd heard about dogs killing sheep, and I believed it after I saw one as big as a wolf down by the creek. It was worse because no dog ever cared if you were in a pumpkin patch when you shouldn't be, but people did, and they might call your parents or the police.

The harder I kept hoping the dog would go away the closer it came. I was glad someone was walking it, but I could tell it wasn't on a leash because it kept jumping around in the gardens, sniffing everything.

I hadn't breathed in about ten minutes and I don't think Bucky had either. We just lay there like we were dead, and I was so afraid it felt like foot-long ants were crawling up and down every inch of me. I wanted to yell when the dog began nosing around the pumpkin patch. It went most of the way around, and we could hear it sniffing, then jumping to some place new and sniffing again.

When it worked its way behind us it sniffed like crazy and rustled the vines and jumped back and forth. Bucky had his face down in the dirt with his hands over his ears like a bomb was getting dropped on him. I still had hold of him but I was looking under my arm, back the way we came. I could see the corn plants moving a little, then again a bit closer as the dog followed us into the patch.

Someone on the sidewalk whistled again but the dog was on us and paid no attention. "C'mon, Potter," a man said, like he was tired. "C'mon!"

It made me feel better that the dog's name wasn't Killer or Fang, or any of the dumb names people give a biting dog. It made me feel worse when the dog suddenly jumped over some vines and landed right behind us. I was so scared I froze and Bucky was so scared he kicked back and popped the dog right in the chops with his sneaker.

The dog jumped so high I lost him against the sky, only to feel him come down right on top of us and go back up again, barking and yelping like a crab was pinched on his nose. Bucky was shaking and I almost peed my pants while the dog crashed through the patch all around us, barking like crazy.

A voice came from across the street, right behind the bang of a screen door. "Get your dog outta that garden!" It was a deep, angry, man voice and it wasn't kidding around, and I thought it was great until the same voice yelled, "Get him out of there or I'll get my shotgun!"

Bucky gripped me harder. I didn't want anyone shooting into the patch with me and Bucky there, even though we were about as tall as a couple of boards, lying all long and flat as we could get.

"Potter, get out of there! Right now!"

That was the stupid dog owner, mad and serious all of a sudden about not wanting to get himself shot. The dumb dog thought he was on to a dinosaur the way he was scrambling around, but he didn't come near us again. I heard the man rustling through the corn, then I heard the kind of yelp you get from a dog that's so busy doing one thing it doesn't notice when you come up on it from behind.

"Dammit, Potter, it's me!" the man said, sounding like he got nipped.

The man dragged his dog away with the other man still yelling, then all of a sudden Bucky tried to get up. I yanked him back down. He tried again and I got on top of him and we made some rustling sounds, then we laid still because making noise was the last thing we wanted to do.

On the sidewalk I could hear the man dragging his dog away, the dog's nails scraping the sidewalk as it tried to get back at us. The owner said, "You got something in there, Mister. Rabbits maybe."

The other man yelled back like he never talked any other way. "If it's a rabbit big enough to eat a pumpkin he's welcome to it!"

We waited a few minutes until the scratching was far off and we heard the screen door bang again. I slid off Bucky and he looked at me without lifting his head off the ground.

I listened real hard to see if I could still hear the dog but I couldn't. I scooted up and pulled on a pumpkin vine, then on another. Bucky crawled past me real fast, I heard a vine snap, then he came back a second later with a bumpy round pumpkin. "I got mine," he said, his voice sounding far off like he was already halfway home.

"It's pretty big," I said.

"I can make it," Buck said, and I knew he would. Once we carried an eight-foot sheet of plywood from the lumber yard all the way to my house, and it was more than a mile. It took half a day but Bucky never quit, even when he got an inch-long sliver in his palm.

I felt a couple pumpkins until I found one with good ridges, a little wider than it was tall, which would be great for a big smiling face. I tried to snap the vine off and leave a stalk, but the stalk snapped off anyway. I was thinking about getting a different pumpkin when we heard a screen door slap again over by the houses.

We scrambled out of the patch and made our way back to the rail yard, staying away from the corn in case the man with the shotgun was waiting to blast away at any sounds. We stopped a few times to rest, but we didn't talk much the whole way back. We heard dog sounds in the weeds along the tracks, and in the shadows in the alley and even in my backyard, and I could still hear them after we got to the house.

We carried the pumpkins most of the way, sometimes rolling them when our arms got tired. In the light from the kitchen window I could see that mine was a little smaller than Buck's, and kinda squashed down like a muffin. We hid them in the garage where the neighbor kids wouldn't find them until after we had a chance to carve them up.

Mom saw us while we were washing our hands in the bathroom sink. "What in the world have you two been doing?" she said, looking at the dirt all over us and the sink and the floor.

"Nothing," I said.

She made both of us take a bath, and by then it was so late we had to go right to bed. Bucky crawled under the blankets on the cot, and I got into bed. Mom tucked us in and turned out the light, and it was only then that I felt how tired I was, and how sore my arms were from carrying that pumpkin.

Bucky said, "You won't tell I was gonna run off, will you?"

I looked over at the cot but I couldn't see him. "No," I said. "I thought about it too."

"Really?" he said.

"Yeah," I said, and I probably would have run off if I hadn't had to hold on to Bucky. I wanted to tell him that but I couldn't see how without sounding chicken.

"Thanks," he said. I heard the cot squeak as he turned over. "I was sure that dog was a werewolf."

A little while later I heard him snoring, while I was still staring at the ceiling.

CORNUCOPIA

~ November ~

Mom pulled into the parking lot at the bus station and shut off the car. Up the street the Summit Bank sign said it was twenty-eight degrees. "Take care of your sister," she said, turning to look at me in the back seat. "You've got Grandma's phone number just in case."

"She'll be there," I said, looking away. "She's always there."

"Are you going to make me apologize forever?" Mom asked. "I said I was sorry."

Mom had been late getting us at Mrs. Wibbley's, so I had to pack my own clothes and help get Megan ready for the bus. I couldn't even find my favorite train pajamas, and I was still mad about it. Mom tried to reach back and tie my hood but I pushed her hands away. "I can do it," I said.

I tied my hood on so tight it hurt my face, 'cause if I didn't Mom would just do it over again. I could see her tying Megan's hood in the front seat, but I couldn't see Megan at all. Megan said, "Okay," when Mom told her to stay with me.

Mom got out, opened the back door on the side

with the suitcases, and I shoved them out to her. The sky was dark gray and it was still windy like it had been all morning. When we walked to the station Mom had me hold Megan's hand so she wouldn't blow over.

I opened the door and held it for Mom and Megan, and then for an old lady with a blue scarf around her head. She was carrying a cornucopia with a blue bow on it.

Mom went over to the ticket counter and put our bags on the scale. I lifted Megan onto one of the ripped old seats so she would watch Mom and leave me alone. With it being so cold out there were a lot of people inside the station, and all the windows were steamed up.

While Mom was paying for the tickets she turned and pointed at us, saying something to the ticket man. He smiled and said something back as he ran the little printing machine over the tickets. Mom came over and handed both of the tickets to me.

"If you need anything you just ask that man right there, okay?" She pointed at the man as he moved our suitcases next to all the others.

I stuffed the tickets in my pocket. "Okay," I said. I was getting hot so I untied my hood and pulled it back. I could feel my hair standing up, all staticky and dry.

"Tell Grandma your father and I will be up Wednesday after work, and I won't forget the pies."

"Pumpkin pie," Megan said, clapping her mittens together.

"That's right, honey. Pumpkin pie with whipped cream." Mom gave her a hug and a kiss. "You be a good girl," she said, checking Megan's coat and mittens, then her coat again.

"Okay."

I tried to walk over by the windows but Mom grabbed my arm. "Are you sure you're going to be all right?"

"Probably," I said.

"Oh, don't do this to me, okay? If you make me any more nervous than I already am you can wait and go up with your dad and me. And you know how disappointed Grandma will be. I have to go to this meeting or you know I'd wait here with you." She checked my coat and tried to pull my hood up but I pushed it back. "Tell me which bus again?" she said.

"Cedar City," I said, like I was stupid. Mom frowned, then gave me a big hug and a kiss. She rubbed her hand over my head, trying to smooth my hair down, but she bent it the wrong way and it hurt. "You're such a big boy so soon," she said.

She gave Megan another hug, then she left, looking back all the way out the door. I wiped some of the steam off a window and watched her get in the car. She didn't go right away, but I couldn't tell what she was doing. It looked like she was just sitting there.

I turned around to make sure Megan was okay, then I looked at all of the people waiting in the station. They mostly looked bored, but a couple of them were kind of creepy too. I didn't want Megan to get worried so I moved over where she could see me at the window.

When I wiped another spot away Mom was gone. A bus pulled in a couple minutes later but it said *CHICAGO* on the front so I went over and looked at the candy machine. The man behind the counter told everybody in the room what cities the Chicago bus was going to, and I hoped a lot of the people were going there and not to Cedar City. Sometimes when the bus was crowded Megan and I had to sit by different people and I didn't like that.

Some of the people headed out to the Chicago bus, but you couldn't tell how many would leave until right at the end 'cause of the smokers and other people who didn't want to get on until the last minute. When our bus came, though, that worked out good for us, because we almost always got on first and got the front seat by the door. You could see out best from there, and nobody could lean a chair back in your face.

Megan said, "Mom, Mom, Mom," and looked around at the people going outside. I walked back over and said, "Mom's gone, Megan. We're going to Grandma's house."

Megan tried to pull her hood back and said, "Gramma's house." I untied her hood and pulled it back, and pulled her zipper down a little because it was digging into her neck.

I heard another bus pull in and the man behind the counter looked out at the parking lot through a side door. I went over and wiped away a new spot on the window, but the bus was hidden behind the Chicago bus so I couldn't see the sign on the front. I felt the tickets in my pocket and then the man behind the counter called out Cedar City.

I grabbed Megan's arm and pulled her off the chair and she fell on her butt. I pulled her up and we headed for the door with all the other people. Somebody held the door for me so we got ahead of a couple more people even though Megan was slowing us down.

Once I got outside I could see the Cedar City bus with its lighted sign, and then I saw the man with the black cane, waiting right by the door of the bus as people got off. I didn't like him because he rode the bus all the time and always tried to hog the front seat. He coughed a lot too, and it seemed like once he got going he couldn't ever stop.

We were right behind the man with the cane when the bus driver came back to the door after unloading people's bags. It was always the same driver. He had gray hair and smoked a pipe, and you always knew it was the right bus more by him than by the sign on the front.

"We're going to Gramma's house," Megan said, and the driver gave her a little smile. A lady got off the bus with about twenty big shopping bags, then the man with the cane tried to get on.

"Hold on a minute," the driver said. "I need to check the bus for belongings."

"I need to use the rest room," said the man with the cane, trying to be quiet, but it was so cold you could hear everything anyway.

"There's one in the depot," said the driver, climbing up the steps.

"Last time I did that I missed the bus," said the man with the cane. He seemed angry about it, too.

The driver came back down the steps and the man with the cane tried stepping up the first step but he even needed help doing that. The bus driver helped him up most of the way, then the man with the cane walked to the back, going so slow I was pretty sure he would have missed the bus again.

The driver followed and they both disappeared to the back. Megan tried climbing up inside but I told her we had to wait for the driver. I heard the bathroom door close and checked my tickets again to make sure we could get on fast since we were first in line.

There were about twenty people behind us, but that didn't count the people waiting in the station until the last minute. The old lady with the cornucopia was halfway back in line and she looked cold. She didn't look like she cared where she was gonna sit though, so I couldn't figure why she didn't wait inside. I pulled Megan's hood up over her head.

The bus driver came back and messed with something by his seat, then came down the steps. When he stepped to the ground I heard the bathroom door open at the back of the bus, then I heard the cane jab into the floor. "Tickets," said the bus driver.

Real fast I pulled our tickets out of my coat and handed them to the driver, 'cause I figured out what the man with the cane was doing. Pretending to have to go to the bathroom was a pretty sneaky way to get the front seat. The driver looked at my ticket like he always did, flipped through the copies like he was lost, then tore the pink one off and handed it back to me.

I could hear the man shuffling up to the front, his cane hitting the floor like he was trying to punch a hole with it. Two shuffles, then the cane again while the bus driver looked over Megan's ticket. The driver tore off the pink copy and I grabbed it and heaved Megan up the steps. "Slow down," he said, when I dropped Megan and she yipped.

I got her up the first few steps and peeked down

the aisle. The man with the cane was standing a few rows back, making a funny face and holding his side. When he looked at me I looked away and pulled Megan up by her arm.

The man with the cane started coming again but I got Megan up in front of me. He stopped and moved to let us go by but I pushed Megan into the front seats by the door. I listened while I helped her into the window seat, but the man with the cane didn't say anything. Then the woman in line behind us climbed up and gave me a smile, and I could hear the man sit down right where he'd been standing, a couple rows back on the other side.

It took a long time for everyone to get on the bus, and for all the bags and coats and things I couldn't figure out to be stuffed on the racks over the seats. The old lady with the cornucopia ended up across the aisle from me, in the window seat behind the driver. The last people getting on didn't have much choice where to sit, but even with the cornucopia in her lap nobody sat beside the old lady. They kept heading to the back even when I was sure there couldn't be any seats left.

When the driver pushed the door closed from the outside and went into the station I knew it wouldn't be long before we left. I unzipped Megan's coat and mine, and pulled her mittens off. I watched for the driver for a minute, then turned and looked down the aisle. The man with the cane was sitting in the aisle seat, his leg and cane stretched out by the seat in front of him, and it didn't look like anyone was sitting by him either. A woman toward the back was putting things up on the rack while her scarf kept flapping in another woman's face. Somebody behind them coughed, and that's when I noticed that the back window was covered up and it was really dark back there.

I wished I'd seen that before 'cause it was a great place to sit, and the covered window only made it better. The only problem was you could never be sure that other people wouldn't sit on the big bench seat with you. Once I got stuck back there between a huge lady in a scratchy dress and a college kid who needed a bath. It was also right by the bathroom door, which was bad if it smelled, and sometimes pretty gross because of the sounds.

When the man with the cane leaned into the aisle to look for the driver I turned around real quick. I didn't think he saw me, but when I peeked to check he was staring right at me so I pretended to look at the floor.

The door opened again and I thought it was going to be the driver, but instead a girl climbed up the steps and looked at the seats. The lady with the cornucopia had put it on the seat beside her, but before she could move it the girl went past toward the back, dragging a big green bag. I didn't look around 'cause I knew the man with the cane would still be staring at me.

The driver came up the steps and closed the door using the big inside handle, then went down the aisle checking the racks. His pipe was in his pocket which meant we were about to go. He disappeared behind us, then I heard him say, "You'll have to move this out of the aisle." A moment later I heard the cane knocking against the seats.

There was some rustling, a girl said, "Thank you,"

then something heavy landed on an overhead rack. There was some more talk I couldn't hear, then someone said, "Cedar City."

The driver came back up front and sat in his seat. He put the girl's ticket with the others on his clipboard and put the clipboard on the dash behind the big door handle. He gave the handle a tug, locking it closed, and put his foot on the brake.

Under the bus something went *fwissshhh…t!*

* * *

It didn't take long to get out of Summit, and by the time we turned on Highway 218 Megan was pointing out all the cows, even though some of them were horses. Then, as soon as the bus got up to highway speed the driver slowed down like he always did and turned off the highway, toward a little town that was really only a couple of buildings.

It was always the same. The bus would drive in and turn around on a little triangle-shaped street. A man in the post office would wave at the driver and he'd wave back, then we'd go back out to the highway. No matter how many trips I made to Grandma's and back, nobody ever got on there and no one ever got off.

Like always we stopped at the railroad tracks that were all grown over on both sides of the road because no train had used them in a hundred years. We turned in at the triangle, like always barely missing the tree and the phone pole, only this time there wasn't even anyone at the post office.

We stopped at the railroad tracks again on the way

out, and the driver looked real hard each way like a bus got hit by a train there that morning. He drove up to the stop sign at the highway and sat there forever, waiting for a bunch of cars that all wanted to turn in front of us at the same time.

Megan was fidgeting so much I pushed her up against the side of the bus. "Don't push me," she said, but she didn't push back so I didn't have an excuse to push her again.

We got out on the highway and I could already see North Branch up the road, where we'd have to turn in again and cross the same railroad tracks, then go past a little grocery store that was never open to see if anybody wanted to get on. Nobody ever got on or off in North Branch, either, and the most I ever saw going on there was a woman walking her cat on a leash, which is also the dumbest thing I ever saw.

The old lady with the cornucopia was looking at me and Megan with a smile, the way old ladies do when you're a kid. I squirmed in my seat a little and thought about Grandma's cornucopia that she puts on the table every Thanksgiving. She has apples and oranges coming out of it, and bananas, and walnuts and other nuts. She says it always stays full no matter how much you take, but if you shake it out on the table nothing happens and you have to put it all back yourself.

The old lady looked out her window at the houses as we went through North Branch. She said something to the driver, who said something back. She sat real still the whole time, even when the bus bounced or rocked back and forth going over the train tracks. I tried it for a while but it was more fun the other way, bouncing all over.

We weren't back on the highway very long before Megan fell asleep. We passed the big gas tanks like the ones that get blown up in war movies, and I scrunched down a little like I always did, just in case. Then we passed the boat place, and right after that the reservoir.

I put Megan's mittens between us and pulled her hood up on her head and down over her eyes. Out past the old lady I could see the trees standing in the reservoir water, which was up pretty high. It was like a whole forest had grown out of the water, but the trees were all bare. It always looked spooky, especially when the water was down and all you could see was black mud and dead trees.

I thought about all the treats Grandma would have, and about playing rummy and building fires in the fireplace, and I was glad school was out. I decided I'd have a root-beer float first thing, unless there was some green Jell-O with pineapple, which you have to eat before a root-beer float or the Jell-O tastes awful.

We went through the woods along the curves and up and down the two hills by the little pond with the island in it. We went down another long hill, then up, and then the bus driver slowed down. Up the road there was a car stopped at the top of the hill, but when we got closer I could see it was a whole line of cars.

The people at the front of the bus saw the line and groaned like Dad does when the football team is losing again. I looked around and the people in back were peeking over their seats to see what everyone up front was looking at, then they started in too. The man with the cane had fallen asleep and he'd put the cane back in the aisle by his leg. One of his eyes wasn't all the way shut, and the way his head was tilted his cheek hung down like the pouch on a kangaroo.

The bus moved up a little, and way up ahead I could see a big line of cars coming toward us down the next hill. Somebody close said, "What now?"

The cars going down the hill in front of us were hardly moving, but the cars coming up at us from the bottom were going fast again. I wasn't sure where we were for a minute, but when the bus moved ahead a bit more I could see the flashing yellow stoplight hanging over the intersection at the bottom of the hill.

The bus driver inched ahead, so close to the car in front of us that I could only see its top. At the bottom of the hill, way at the front of the line of cars, a big gas truck pulled over to the side of the road and I could see it was going around some cars in the middle of the intersection.

I leaned up and rested my chin on the bar in front of our seat. It was cold so I put my hands on the bar under my chin, but then my hands got cold so I pulled them inside my coat sleeves.

When the gas truck headed up the other side of the hill I could see two police cars. They were sitting on the gravel on our side of the road, their lights flashing. A policeman was directing traffic under the yellow light.

When we got closer I could make out two cars sitting in the intersection. A green car had smashed into the side of a white car, and the white one looked like Bucky's dump truck after he stuck it under the back wheel of his mom's car.

People in the cars coming up the hill were looking back behind them. When I turned to see if the man with the cane was looking it turned out everybody on the bus was looking and they all ended up looking at me. "Get out of the way," somebody said, so I turned around and leaned on the cold bar again. The old lady looked at me with a sad face, then looked down at her hands in her lap.

Another policeman climbed out of the green car holding a blanket. He walked to the white car, then leaned down beside it and disappeared.

When we got closer I could see the back of another car I hadn't seen before. It was sticking out of the ditch on the other side of the road. All around the intersection there was busted glass and pieces of cars. On our side of the road there was a whole chrome bumper, all bent and twisted like the fender on my bike after I tore it off.

The policeman stood up again and leaned on the side of the white car. He took off his hat and rubbed his hair, looking up the road toward Cedar City. Then he covered his face with his hand and didn't move.

When we got close enough I could see two people sitting in the open doors of the police cars. They both looked like they had bloody noses. I looked at Megan and she was awake, looking out the side window at the fields.

As we drove around the cars and bounced along the edge of the ditch I could see a blanket lying on the ground by the green car, and another blanket covering up the driver's seat of the white car. The policeman leaning on the car looked up as we went by and his face was all red.

We got through the intersection and started up the hill, then we had to slow down again and ease over by the ditch because an ambulance was coming toward us in our lane. Megan saw the flashing lights and said, "Fire truck." The whole bus felt like a library all of a sudden and I could hear myself breathing.

"It's an ambulance," I said, real quiet.

I looked over at the old lady, who had put the cornucopia back on her lap. She looked sick and I could see her eyes were wet like she was getting ready to cry. I thought maybe she knew some of the people sitting in the police cars.

"It's so terrible," she said, looking at me.

The driver said, "I've written two letters about that light in the past three years."

The old lady kept looking at me, holding her cornucopia real tight. "I hope they weren't children," she said, then she started to cry so I looked out the window with Megan.

"I don't think so," the driver said.

*   *   *

Grandma was waiting for us when we got to the Cedar City station. We were the first ones off and she was right there. She gave us big hugs and pulled our hoods up, tying them tight. Grandma picked Megan up in her arms.

We walked back to the side of the bus where the driver was unloading the bags. Grandma said, "How was your trip?" and I could see her looking at the people as they got off the bus all quiet and sad.

"Okay," I said.

At Grandma's house we had root beer floats first, but Grandma promised she'd make green Jell-O with pineapple for dinner. We played cards for a while, even though Megan only helps Grandma, then Grandma gave Megan a bath.

I went into the dining room and looked at the cornucopia. It was where it always was, in the middle of the table, and there were big apples and oranges and bananas spilling out of it, and acorns and walnuts. I got close and smelled them all. I watched to see if more stuff was coming out of it, but nothing moved until I shook it a little and an apple rolled across the table and almost fell off.

Grandma came down and said Megan was sleeping. She said we needed logs for the fire Thanksgiving morning, so I put on my mittens and coat and went out the back door.

It was dark, but there was light on the wood pile from a streetlight in the alley. I could see my breath in the light, and I could feel how much colder it was.

I pulled the cover off the wood pile and pulled out some logs. Some of them were pretty heavy so it took a couple trips before I thought there was enough on the back porch to last. I brushed the rotten bark off my coat and pulled the cover back over the wood to make sure it wouldn't get wet.

The streetlight threw my shadow on the cover. I tried to make shadow animals with my hands but they just looked like mittens. I jumped so I could see that my shadow feet were off the ground, then I turned sideways to see my breath make a shadow but it didn't.

I looked at the cover and I thought about the old lady crying on the bus. The wind was burning my ears so I pulled my hood up. Overhead I watched some low clouds blow by, yellow from the city lights.

It was cold, but I stayed there, looking at the cover whipping in the wind, until Grandma called out the back door. Before I went in I touched the cover again, feeling the logs underneath.

BOYS

~ December ~

"Hey, Buck."

"What?"

"You awake?"

"Yeah."

I rolled over in bed and peeked out the side under my quilt. I could see the cot, and the blankets piled all over it, but I couldn't see Bucky anywhere. "You look like a big worm," I said.

The blankets moved a little, then I saw Bucky's face in a little cave at the edge. "So do you," he said, then he closed the cave back up. "It's cold in here."

I'd been thinking the same thing since I woke up. I ducked back under the blankets and flipped over, looking out the other side. I was gonna look out the window to see if it had snowed but the window was covered with frost.

I stuck a hand out to feel if the frost was on the inside or outside and one of my fingernails scratched it, sending a shiver all the way down my back. I yanked my arm in and curled into a ball. "I think the heater vent's closed," I said.

"Open it," Buck said, all muffled under the blankets.

"You're closer," I said. "The thing that holds it up is busted. It falls down sometimes."

"It's your vent."

I got another shiver thinking about how the frost felt under my fingernails. "I'm warm enough," I said.

"Me too," Buck said

I tried to think what would get him to open the vent but I couldn't think of anything. I made a little air hole at the edge of the blankets 'cause it was getting stuffy, then I thought about all the toys I got at Christmas, and how maybe we could set up the race track we were working on so it would do more tricks.

"Hey, Buck."

"What?"

"You believe in Santa Claus?"

"Yeah. Why?"

"Lyle Gant said there isn't any Santa Claus."

"Lyle's a liar. If he said his sister loved you would you believe it?"

"You bet." Kayla Gant was in sixth grade. She was pretty, and the first girl I ever kissed. "Wouldn't you?" I said.

"Nah. She wouldn't love me."

Bucky had come over after we got back from Christmas at Grandma's. He was gonna stay with us a few days while his mom went out of town to see his dad. I couldn't figure out why they didn't want Buck there too, and when I asked Mom all she said was it was a good question.

Megan was staying at Grandma's while Buck was

staying with us, which woulda made it twice as good except Bucky'd been pretty quiet since he'd come over, and every time I tried to cheer him up he said something mopey. "You think he lives at the North Pole?" I said.

"Where else is he gonna live?"

"I don't know. It's just a long way is all. I mean, how's he gonna do everything he does all in one night like that? I can't even get my homework done in one night."

"That's 'cause you're so dumb. If you had as many elves as he does you'd get your homework done." And that was a great idea. I tried thinking about how I could get some elves but Bucky kept talking and I got lost trying to listen and think at the same time. "Another thing he's got is magic. Going up chimneys and stuff. It's not like he has to do everything like we do it. Load everything in a car and go somewhere and unload it, or wait around for his mom to pick him up. He just touches his nose."

"I think I'll push Lyle in the snow," I said, still trying to think about elves doing my homework. "Hey, it'd be like those shoemakers!"

"What shoemakers?"

"You know, those little elves that make that guy's shoes all night 'cause he's too tired. In the book. If we could get them to do our homework maybe they'd clean our rooms. Maybe even eat stuff we didn't want!"

Bucky said, "Lima beans!" all muffled under his blanket, and I laughed because it was just what I was thinking.

"Open the heater vent, okay?" I said.

"Open it yourself."

I jumped out of bed and yanked Bucky's covers off, but he was wrapped inside so he fell on the floor. I jumped back in bed but I was laughing so hard I almost fell out again.

I thought Bucky would try to pull my covers off so I was holding them real tight, but instead he jumped right on me with a yell. He got me good with something bony right in my back, but when I tried to kick him through the blankets my legs got tangled in the sheet.

"Get off!"

"You started it!"

"I can't breathe!"

"You're lyin'," Buck said, bouncing on me like I was a big pillow. I heard something I couldn't figure out, then Buck stopped bouncing and got off the bed. I thought he was waiting to attack me, but then the blankets peeled back and I was looking at Dad in his big red robe.

"Think you could hold it down?" he said. Bucky was standing by his cot looking a little worried, but I could tell Dad wasn't mad. "I want your mother to sleep in as long as she can. We wore her out pretty good this year."

Mom and Grandma always cooked a lot at Christmas, making big dinners and cookies and mints and fudge and divinity and peanut brittle, and some stuff I could never remember the name of. Then they made more stuff and took it to Grandma's neighbors, then later the neighbors would come over and give us something they made. "Maybe she's sick," I said.

"No, she's not sick. Just tired. Let's go downstairs,

quietly, and I'll make some waffles." I could see Bucky cheer up when Dad said waffles. "Why is it so cold in here?" he said, looking at the heater vent. Dad pulled his robe tight and tied the belt again. "I thought I fixed that."

"Maybe it broke again," I said.

"Maybe it did," he said, then he slapped me on the butt and ran me out the door. Right after that I heard Bucky squeal and he came running out after me.

We ran down the hall and down the stairs, forgetting to be quiet until we heard Dad say "Shhh!" I tiptoed to the kitchen, thinking about waffles, but in the living room I saw the race track and what we'd done the night before, and I got a great idea.

"Hey, Buck," I said. "What if we put a big curlycue in it, like the slide at the swimming pool? That'd use up some of the left turns."

Buck looked at the kitchen. "What about the waffles?"

"Dad'll tell us when they're done." Bucky looked at Dad walking into the kitchen like he was gonna get gypped, but I could see him thinking about the track again too. "A curlicue off a table or something," I said. "Then maybe a loop before it goes in the dining room."

"We could do it off the kitchen table," Buck said. "The cars'd get a good start. Maybe we could get 'em going fast enough for two loops."

We'd never gotten a car through two loops before. The way it worked, you put all the track together how you wanted it, then you put a car in the track at the high end and let it go. It had to go pretty fast if the track was real long, and if you put a loop too far at the end the car might only go halfway around and fall off upside down. It was funny, and sometimes we planned it that way, but with the new track and cars we both got we were trying to make the biggest track ever.

We asked Dad about using the kitchen table and he said it was okay, so we got a bunch of the left turns and made a double curlicue. When we first clamped it to the table it twisted too much, but then Buck put one of the kitchen chairs under the first curl and it worked great. The track even came out between the legs of the chair before shooting out into the living room.

We tried a couple cars and they went real fast. We put a jump at the end in the dining room, and we were gonna set up two loops, but right then Dad came out and said, "Who wants a waffle?" Bucky's hand went up like it was tied to a jet.

"We're all out of maple syrup, so we're going to have to use this, okay?" Dad showed us a bottle of fake syrup that had been in the fridge for about a hundred years.

"I don't care," Buck said.

"There's maple syrup," I said. "Up in the cupboard."

"I don't think so," Dad said. "I just looked."

I went past Dad into the kitchen, pulled out a drawer and climbed up on the counter. Dad said, "That was probably the old one you saw." I walked across the stove and stepped over the waffle iron and opened the cupboard. "I don't think your mom bought any more," he said, and at first I couldn't see it 'cause somebody'd moved it, but then I saw it way in the back behind the salt. It was a brand new bottle.

"I knew it was in here," I said. "I saw it before we went to Grandma's."

"Great," said Dad, putting me on the floor and taking the bottle. He looked at the fake syrup, then threw it in the garbage.

Bucky was sitting at the table, watching the steam come out the sides of the waffle iron. Dad poured some syrup into a pan to heat it up and had me get the milk and butter. I made Bucky pour the milk while I took a long time unwrapping the butter.

The steam stopped coming out of the waffle iron and Dad opened it, burning his fingers like he always does. The waffle stuck to the top and we could see it was dark brown and crunchy, which is the way Bucky and me decided they're best.

Dad was prying the waffle loose with a fork when the phone rang in the living room. He fumbled with the fork and the phone rang again, then he grabbed the waffle with his hand and burned his fingers again. He tried getting it on a plate in one big piece but the bottom two squares fell off and landed on his bare foot.

The phone rang again and Dad cursed and threw all the squares on a plate while Buck and me sat waiting at the table with butter on our knives. Dad took a couple quick steps toward the living room but the phone quit in the middle of a ring. He stopped in the doorway and slapped the wall.

Dad came back, almost tripping over our track, and gave us the plate of waffles. He poured more batter in the waffle iron and closed the lid, but he put too much in and a big blob came out the side. He gave us the warm maple syrup in a little pitcher and I could see him looking at the ceiling. Then I heard the bathroom door shut and I knew Mom was getting up and that didn't seem to make Dad any happier.

"Boy, these are good," Buck said.

"Thank you, Bucky," Dad said, still listening to Mom upstairs. Bucky looked at me and I looked back at him and shrugged my shoulders. He shrugged his shoulders back and for a minute we both shrugged our shoulders until Dad put another batch of waffles on the plate.

We got through another couple waffles each and then the phone rang again. This time Dad said, "Son of a bitch," and was out in the living room before it stopped ringing once.

I could hear him talking real quiet, and I thought maybe Mom went back to bed, but when I looked up from finishing my milk she was standing in the kitchen door in her nightgown. Buck saw her about the same time I did, and we both got the creeps because it looked like she'd been crying. "How're the waffles?" she said, looking over at the waffle iron, which was still steaming a bit.

When we didn't say anything she moved toward the waffle iron, but she didn't see our track and tripped on it and almost fell down. The track got ripped off the table and one of Bucky's cars went sliding under the fridge.

"I'm sorry," she said. She picked up the end of the track that had been clamped to the table, but she didn't see the clamp lying under the chair, so when she went to hook it back on the table there wasn't any way for her to do it. She just stood there, touching the track to the table, and then she started crying.

Buck was looking straight down and I was pretty much too, then I saw Dad come into the kitchen and take the track out of Mom's hand and drop it on the floor. He gave Mom a big hug and said, "You boys go upstairs and play awhile."

We got out of the kitchen real fast and raced upstairs and back into our beds under all the blankets. I curled up and listened but there wasn't anything to hear. I wished Bucky wasn't staying with us so I could be alone.

"When is your mom coming back?" I said.

"Day after tomorrow," Bucky said under his blankets.

"Think she'll bring you something?"

"I don't know. Like what?"

"I don't know. Something fun."

"I don't know," he said. He didn't say anything for a minute, then he said, "My mom cries sometimes."

I peeked out the side of the blankets at Buck's cot. His covers were up in the middle like a tent, and I could tell he was on his back with his legs up. I rolled over and did the same thing, and when I pushed my legs straight up a bunch of cold air came whooshing in through the hole I'd been looking out. "Want to play Monopoly?" I said.

"Nah. Takes too long."

"How about cards?"

"What'cha got?"

"Just regular cards."

"My mom showed me how to play Old Maid with a regular deck once, but I can't remember it," Bucky said. "You have to get rid of some of the cards I think."

"We have an old maid deck up at Grandma's," I said, wishing I'd stayed up there with Megan. "How about coloring? I still got that poster to finish."

"Nah. I don't feel like it."

It was getting hot under the blankets so I pushed the covers up and down till it cooled off, then I closed the hole. I heard the cot squeak, and all of a sudden I was pretty sure Buck was going to jump on me again so I coiled my legs. When I felt him touch the blankets I kicked out and got him pretty good.

I laughed and scrambled out from under the covers before he could get me again, but Buck was sitting on his cot, the blankets around him like a big cape. Dad was standing by my bed holding a corner of my quilt. His other hand was holding his coffee cup away from him, and he was watching coffee run down the front of his robe.

"Guess I shouldn't have sneaked up on you, " he said, like it was funny, but he wasn't smiling. Bucky laughed and I was glad he was there. Dad sat down on the edge of my bed, rubbing the spilled coffee into his robe.

"I wanted to tell you why your mother was upset. One of her students called to tell her he decided to join the army. He's a good student and your mother had hopes for what he might become. Now she's afraid he'll get killed over there but there's nothing she can do."

Bucky and I sat still while he took a sip of coffee. You can tell when Dad's done talking and he wasn't done talking. I pulled my quilt up around me and Dad looked at the heater vent again like it was making fun of him.

"I don't know why he wants to go." he said, rubbing his forehead like he does when he's serious about something. "I don't know if *he* knows why he wants to go. Men have been going to war for a long time, and women have been crying over them just as long, and none of it's going to stop now."

Dad smiled at me and Bucky and reached over and messed up Bucky's hair. "Maybe we'll figure it out so you boys don't have to do anything but grow up." He paused again, looking at us and drinking his coffee. "So if Mom's upset, that's why. It's got nothing to do with you, okay?"

"Okay," I said. I looked at Bucky but he didn't look like he knew what Dad was talking about any better than me. Dad got up and looked at the heater vent for a minute, then propped it open with a Tinker Toy stick. "Come on down and finish those waffles now," he said.

Buck was off his cot in a second, and I went down too even though I was pretty full. I looked in Mom's room on the way down and I could see she was back in bed facing the wall. I wanted to go in and see her but I didn't think I should.

We ate the rest of the waffles and it about made me sick. We worked on the track awhile, and watched some TV, and Mom came down and sat with us on the couch. She put her arms around both of us and we sat real still because we didn't want her to cry again.

Mom said, "I'm sorry if I scared you."

"No," I said, hoping she wouldn't say anything

else.

She gave me a big hug and laughed, and for a minute I was scared she was going to cry but she didn't. "What would you like to do today?" she said, wiping her eyes like we wouldn't notice.

"I don't know," I said.

"Make cookies," Bucky said, and I woulda slugged him only Mom was in the way. I was trying to decide between putt-putt golf and bowling and a movie and a whole bunch of other stuff and all Buck could think of was more food.

"Okay," Mom said. "Cookies it is."

*   *   *

We made the cookies after the TV show was over, and when we were done I asked if we could go bowling anyway. Mom said yes but Dad was there too and he said no. I tried asking again later but Dad got mad and told us to go play outside. We woulda been in more trouble but Mom said it was too cold for us to go outside and she didn't want any tension in the house.

We spent most of the rest of the day in my room, helping Dad fix the heater vent, and playing Monopoly with a bunch of our own made-up rules. Bucky got a call from his mom after dinner and she said she was gonna be gone for another couple days. I didn't know he was mad about it until we were getting ready for bed and he said he hoped she never came back.

Mom got more phone calls too, then she went to bed before we did so we had to be quiet. When Dad said it was bedtime I let Buck have my bed and I took the cot. I got my quilt though 'cause it was from my grandma, and I took my pillow.

We talked for a while after Dad tucked us in and turned out the lights. Buck said he wished his mom was coming home when she said she was gonna be home the first time, and I thought about Mom crying and it made me mad at the guy that was going in the army. "If that guy gets killed he deserves it," I said.

"What guy?"

"The guy goin' in the army. The guy Mom was crying about. If he gets killed it's his own stupid fault."

Bucky said, "Think your mom would cry if you were going?"

"Yeah. She'd cry a lot. She cries at the Wizard of Oz when Dorothy gets to go home at the end."

"I think my mom'd cry if my dad was going," he said.

We were quiet a while and I got thinking about being in a war when Buck said, "If there's a war for us are you gonna go?"

"I don't know," I said. "You?"

"I don't know."

"If you go I'd probably go."

"What if I don't?"

"I don't know. Maybe I'd go."

"Why?"

"I don't know."

It was quiet for a little bit.

"Night," Bucky said.

"Night."

"Night."

"Night."

"Night."

"Shut up."

"You shut up."

"I'd go if I got to be a fighter pilot," I said.

"On an aircraft carrier!" Bucky said, and he made a zooming sound under his covers.

"That'd be great," I said, and I thought about shooting off a carrier deck and pulling up into the sky. I'd look back over my shoulder at the carrier getting smaller and smaller and smaller, and fly up into the moonlight, rolling and looping and whooshing past the clouds.

I looked at the window by my bed. The frost was gone, but the glass was glowing from the streetlight outside. "Night," I said.

"Night," Bucky said.

"Night."

"Night."

"Night."

"Night."

"Night."

GLASS

~ January ~

The man on the radio coughed. "Excuse me," he said. "Classes at Tanama are canceled, as are those at Lakeside. Long Valley Schools will begin one hour late. Brookside School District has canceled classes."

I watched the snow falling outside the living room window. The flakes were big and fluffy and there wasn't any wind at all. "Tonight's meeting of Sisters' Weaving Club is canceled. The Ballroom Association Dance has moved to next Monday, provided it stops snowing by then. The Senior Citizens Art Fair has been postponed."

On her way into the kitchen Mom stopped in the living room with Megan on her hip and turned the radio up. I looked out at a big branch on the maple tree in the front yard. It was covered with a foot of snow on top, but on the sides the bark looked like it did in summer. A squirrel ran past, hanging on to the bottom of the branch, then went into a hole in the trunk. A moment later it stuck its head out and looked around like I was looking around.

"Summit School District has canceled classes for

today."

"Mom!"

"I heard," Mom said from the kitchen, sounding tired. She came out and shut the radio off, then looked out past me at the snow.

The phone rang. "I'll get it!" I said.

"*I'll* get it," Mom said, pulling it off the hook just before I got there. She said hello, then I could hear Bucky's voice on the line. "Just a minute," she said, handing me the phone. "It's Bucky."

I grabbed the phone and Mom went back to the kitchen. "Did you hear?"

"Yeah!" Bucky yelled. "No school!"

"Let's go sledding!"

"Hang on," Buck said, and I could hear him talking to his mom for a second. "It's okay if you can come over here," he said, "but Mom can't bring me over there and she doesn't want me walkin' over."

"Hang on," I said, stretching around the corner to the kitchen. "Mom, can I go over to Bucky's and go sledding?"

"Sure," Mom said, filling a bowl with milk and cereal. She set it in front of Megan, who was coloring a piece of paper at the table. "Just be home for lunch."

To the phone I said, "I'll meet you at the hill after breakfast."

"Okay!" Buck said and hung up.

I hung up, went into the kitchen, sat down in front of my bowl, and poured out the rest of the cereal box. I could tell Mom was tired because I got three tablespoons of sugar on my cereal before she stopped me.

"I want to go," Megan said.

I could see Mom was thinking about it so I said, "You'll get cold and want to come home."

"No I won't," Megan said, sticking out her tongue.

"Yes you will," I said. "You'll get frozen solid and I'll have to pull you all the way back like a block of ice."

"I want to go!" Megan yelled, smacking her bowl with her spoon and slopping milk and cereal all over the table.

"Megan, stop that!" Mom said, grabbing her arm. "It's too cold out for you."

"I want to go!" she yelled, sliding down in her chair and kicking the table leg. Mom pulled her back up and held her still, then turned and looked at me. "Maybe you better stay home too," she said.

"But Bucky's waiting," I said, kicking at Megan's chair under the table. "I gotta go."

Megan tried throwing herself on the floor but Mom pulled her up and picked pieces of cereal off Megan's shirt. To Megan she said, "We'll make muffins, okay?" Megan hugged Mom and stuck her tongue out again. I poured milk on my cereal and didn't look up while I ate.

*　*　*

I had my warmest sledding clothes on, including plastic bread bags over my feet inside my boots, so they wouldn't get wet even if they got cold. I got the two-person toboggan out of the garage and pulled it through the backyard into the alley. The snow was falling so thick I could hardly see to the end at the street.

I heard a car spin its wheels, then a bang, then

everything got quiet again. I stopped and listened, trying to figure out what the bang was. I watched the snow falling again and it made me feel quiet. I tried to see if I could hear the snow hitting the ground but I couldn't.

When I got to the end of the alley I saw that a car had smashed into the side of a parked car on the other side of the street. A man was standing by the cars, looking at where they hit.

The porch door opened on a little house up from the cars and a man in a robe leaned out. "How bad is it?" he said.

"I couldn't stop," the other man said. "It's not too bad."

"Dammit," said the man in the robe, quietly closing the door and going back inside.

The man by the cars saw me, looked at my toboggan, then said, "Enjoy it while it lasts, kid." I turned where the sidewalk was, even though I couldn't see it under all the fresh snow, and pretended I was skating until I got to Summit Street.

A few cars had gone by but no plows, so the snow was as thick and white in the streets as it was everywhere else. I heard a train rumbling by down at the tracks, and when I looked I could see smoke and heat puffing up from under the bridge.

Behind me the man in the robe had come back out wearing an unbuckled pair of boots. He was cursing the other man and his car, but the other man just leaned on his fender and scratched his head. The man in the robe put his hands on his hips, then turned and yelled back at a woman who stuck her head out the door. "No we don't want any coffee!"

I crossed Summit and walked the next block in the street, then cut through the yard by the old-folk's home, through the hole in the back fence, and across the schoolyard. Even in the falling snow I thought I could see fresh tracks coming across the field from the direction of Bucky's house. When I got to the top of the hill I saw Buck coming up, pulling his runner sled behind him like a submarine in the deep snow.

Bucky saw me and smiled and slipped and fell on his face, almost disappearing in the thick snow himself. When his head popped up he had a big grin. "It's deep!" he yelled.

"We'll have to mash it down," I said.

"I know," Bucky said, getting up again. When he got to the top we stood looking down the hill. "It's quiet," he said.

"Yeah," I said. "I never heard it this quiet before."

I put my toboggan at the top of the hill and Bucky got on, holding the handles on the sides. I pulled the toboggan ahead and down the hill, flattening the snow so the runners on Buck's sled wouldn't get stuck. Bucky leaned from side to side to keep the track even, and when too much snow got piled in front I kicked it out of the way.

"A guy ran his car into a parked car on Bowery," I said.

"You see it?"

"No, I heard it though. Didn't sound like what it was, like it does on TV. Sounded like somebody dropping a dirt clod in a bucket."

When we got about halfway down Bucky got off and I sat down. Bucky pulled hard on the rope and I fell over backwards and we both laughed. I got back on the toboggan and Bucky said, "I told Mom I'd come home for lunch but I'm not gonna."

"You can come over to my house," I said.

"Okay," Buck said, pulling me down the rest of the hill. "She said it's too cold to be out long."

"It ain't cold," I said.

"I know," Bucky said, pushing me into the snow. "Race you to the top!"

I got up and chased him, and even pulling the toboggan I caught him about halfway up. I tackled him and rubbed his face in the snow, then ran up the rest of the way.

When Bucky caught up I thought for a minute he was mad, but then he hit me in the face with a bunch of snow he was hiding. "Truce," he said.

"Truce," I said, wiping snow out of my nose and picking up the toboggan rope. "Let's go together until it gets fast."

"Okay," Bucky said.

I put the toboggan at the top of the new run and sat in front, cross-legged. Bucky got behind with his legs around me on top of my legs. We pushed over the lip of the hill, paddling with our arms, but we didn't get going much the whole way down 'cause the snow was still too thick.

At the bottom Bucky rolled off on his back and stared up at the falling snow. "You think snowflakes are really all different?" he said.

I looked up at the snow falling down on me from everywhere. "I guess so," I said, then I looked at the snow all over the field, and on the roofs of the houses across the alley. "Like anybody could ever find two alike anyway."

Bucky rolled over on his side and looked at the snow real close. I started back up the hill with the toboggan, walking on the path to flatten it down more. I was halfway up when Bucky yelled, "I found 'em!"

Without looking back I yelled, "You did not!"

"Dang, they melted," Bucky said.

"Come on!" I yelled when I got to the top. I put the toboggan in the track again and sat down. Sliding back and forth I could feel the snow getting faster. "This is gonna be great," I said as Bucky came up.

"Let's take my sled this time," he said.

"It's still too deep for the runners," I said.

"I'll go down myself."

"Just get on back."

"Let me sit up front."

"I pulled it back up," I said. "Whoever brings the sled up gets to choose."

Bucky slumped. "Oh yeah," he said, then he got on behind and we pushed off again. The toboggan got going pretty good, then we drifted into fresh snow and slowed down a bit. "Watch where you're goin'!" Buck yelled.

"I am!" I yelled, leaning the other way and getting the toboggan back on track.

We got going pretty fast about halfway down, then we really got going. When we got to the end of the run and hit thick snow again the toboggan stopped and we flew over the front. Bucky landed on top of me, then jumped up and yelled, "That was great!"

I got up and turned around, trying to shake the

snow out of my mittens and collar. Bucky took the toboggan and headed back up the hill. I made a snowball and threw it at Buck but I missed and he didn't see it go by. I made another and ran up a little closer and hit him right in the back.

Bucky turned around. "We had a truce!" he said.

"I thought that was only for pushing," I said.

Bucky kicked a bunch of snow at me and started up the hill again. I made another snowball and threw it and missed, but he saw that one go by. "Cut it out," he said, not looking back.

I made another snowball and packed it real tight, then I threw it up so it would come straight down on his head. It went so high I lost it in the falling snow, but it seemed like a good throw. "Heads!" I yelled.

Bucky put his free arm over his head and ducked. If he hadn't moved it probably would have missed him, but it hit him right in the back of the neck. Buck turned around and I could see he was mad. "Cut it out or I'm goin' home!"

"Okay," I said.

Bucky pulled the toboggan up the rest of the way, then put his runner sled in the track. He sat down in front, holding the rope, waiting for me to get to the top. When I did he was looking across the field at something. "Who's that?" he said.

I looked where he was pointing, and through the snow I could see three big kids coming out the back of a house across the field. Two of them had blue coats on and the other one was wearing a green coat and a red headband. They were throwing snow at each other and running for the field. "I don't know," I said.

"It's Pelican," Bucky said, standing up over his sled, holding tight on the rope.

Pelican is what everybody calls Dave Pelleck because of his big nose, which is bigger than anybody's nose I've ever seen, including grownups. Pelican was a grade ahead, which was also why nobody called him Pelican to his face except Rodney Garner, who was in Pelican's grade but got held back a year.

"Huh-uh," I said. "Pelican's coat is red with white checks." I didn't want it to be Pelican because he stole Bucky's sled once and wouldn't give it back until Dad came to get us.

Bucky kept watching the kids as they ran across the alley and down the hill into the field. "Maybe he got a new coat for Christmas," Bucky said.

The two kids in the blue coats jumped on the kid in the green coat, and for a minute the kid in the green coat was sideways and you could see it was Pelican even all the way across the field in the falling snow. I walked over and grabbed the rope on my toboggan.

"That's the Drury brothers with him," I said.

The Drurys are the dumbest kids ever to go to our school, including Mike Craig. After Lance Drury got caught smoking Lyle Drury got caught shoplifting, then they both got caught stealing bikes from the racks right in front of the school.

"Let's go," Bucky said.

"Where?"

"Anywhere," Buck said. The Drury brothers were fighting each other, which is when Pelican noticed us and started running right for us.

"He's comin'!" I said, and we ran for the hole in

the fence behind the old-folk's home. Bucky went first and for a minute he got his sled stuck but I shoved it through after him.

When I pushed through the fence I turned around and saw Pelican standing at the top of the hill, looking at me. "Come on!" Bucky yelled, running away. I ran after him, and we didn't stop running until we were halfway to Summit Street.

A snowplow had gone by on Summit and cleared one side of the street. We looked back but couldn't see Pelican, so we crossed without trying to lose him first. The car that had run into the parked car was gone, and there was a big dent in the side of the parked car.

"That's the car that got hit," I said.

Bucky stopped ahead of me to look at the dent. "I wish I saw it happen," he said.

"Yeah, me too," I said. I waited for Buck to get going again but he didn't move. "Let's go down to the tracks."

"Okay," Bucky said, but he still didn't move.

"C'mon, Buck – get goin'!"

When he still wouldn't move I stepped around his sled to shove him off the walk, but then I heard it too. A snowplow was working somewhere, and it sounded like it was getting closer.

Behind us a car turned onto Bowery from Summit and I couldn't hear the plow anymore. As the car drove by the driver looked at me and Buck like we were two dumb penguins standing there. For a minute I thought the driver might smash into the dented car because he wasn't looking where he was going, but he didn't. Instead, he drove down to the stop sign at the corner, turned right and disappeared.

A second later, right where I was looking, the front end of a big yellow city plow popped out at the corner a block down on Lucas. After a pause, the plow turned toward us, and Bucky looked back at me with a big smile on his face. "I wish I could drive one of those."

"Yeah," I said. "Me too."

The plow stopped at the stop sign on my street and I thought it might turn one way or the other, but after another pause it came straight at us, scraping up snow and piling it on the curb. We waved at the driver and he waved back, then gave us a long, loud honk on his horn as he went by, throwing a spray of snow on our legs and sleds.

The plow paused at the stop sign at Summit, then crossed and headed down Bowery toward school. "That was neat," Bucky said, still smiling.

I pulled my toboggan around Bucky and headed down to my street. Behind me I could hear Bucky following, making noises like he was plowing the sidewalk.

When we were almost at my house Bucky said, "Let's ask your mom for some hot chocolate."

"We better not," I said, thinking how good hot chocolate would be. "She might make us take Megan with us when we go back out. Besides, we don't have any marshmallows."

"I don't care," Bucky said, but I kept walking past my house. A few cars had driven down the street, so I went out and walked in a tire track where it was easier. Buck caught up in another track and then we walked backwards, watching the different patterns our sleds made in the snow outside the tire tracks.

"Nobody'll ever figure out what made these," I said.

"We can say it was spacemen," Bucky said, and I thought that was the dumbest thing he ever said.

"Spacemen don't drive around in the snow," I said.

"You think they're just gonna fly down the middle of the street?" Bucky said. "They would try to blend in. Maybe even drive around in a fake city plow."

It was such a creepy thought that I looked to see if any of the tire tracks went to my house, even though I knew they didn't. Right then Dad stepped out on the porch and looked up and down the street. When he saw us he yelled, "Bucky!" and waved us back.

Bucky looked at Dad and said, "What'd I do?" He looked at me and said, "I didn't do anything."

We went back all slow and mopey and Dad met us by the curb. "Bucky, your mom wants you home. She went over to get you at the field but you weren't there and now she's pretty upset."

"Right now?" Bucky said, and I could tell he was thinking about Pelican and the Drury brothers.

"Right now," Dad said.

Bucky's mom was never in a good mood anyway, but Pelican and the Drurys were worse. I said, "Can you give Buck a ride home, Dad? We wrecked pretty good and his leg's sore."

Dad looked at the snow in the street and on the car in the driveway, then up at the snow falling on his head. "Sure," he said. "You coming?"

"No. I'm gonna keep sleddin'. See ya Buck."

"Bye," Bucky said, like school had started for him and nobody else.

They headed back to the house, Dad carrying Bucky's sled and Bucky kicking snow. I set my toboggan over a tire track again and pulled it down the street to the dead end. When I got to the top of the hill above the tracks there was a big new pile of railroad ties right where we always slid down. The black ties were covered with white snow, but even in the cold the sides were shiny with tar.

I pulled my toboggan up and sat on it. I thought about going down anyway and crashing into the ties, but I didn't. Instead I looked at the ties and thought about Pelican's nose. I thought about how I wanted to be big enough to beat him up, and right in the middle of imagining a bunch of punches I heard diesel engines coming.

I slid down the hill on my butt, then ran around the pile of ties and across the frozen ditch water onto the tracks. Up around the curve an engine light came into view. As it slowly turned toward me it cut through the falling snow and reflected off two shiny bare spots on the rails under the Summit Street bridge.

I kicked some snow off the ballast beside the main line and grabbed as many loose rocks as I could with my mittens. The train was getting louder, and from how hard the engines were pulling I knew it was a big freight.

Running back across the ditch ice one of my boots cracked through an air pocket and I almost fell down. I looked up the tracks and the engine light was getting brighter. I picked up a couple of the rocks I dropped and ran around the back of the ties.

When I counted the rocks I only had eight so I ran back out and jumped the ditch to get more. I pulled one mitten off and stuffed some rocks in my pockets and got more in my arms and then the train whistle blew. I looked up and the lead engine was at the bridge.

I jumped back across the ditch and didn't stop for any of the rocks I dropped. I ducked behind the ties again, then I remembered my toboggan sitting out in the open at the top of the ravine. I dropped the rocks in my hands and put my mitten back on, but the hill was slick and I kept sliding back down until I found clumps of dead weeds to grab under the snow.

I got to the top and reached for my toboggan right as a wall of snow came at me from the street. Behind the snow I saw the big blade of a city plow, and in the yellow cab above I saw the same driver who honked at me and Bucky. Even with the plow almost on top of me the train engines were so loud I couldn't hear the blade scraping the street.

Right when I thought the plow was going to shove the snow pile down the hill and me along with it, the driver saw me and slammed his brakes like Mom does when she almost runs over a squirrel. I grabbed the rope on my toboggan and kicked my way down the hill head first, on the back of my coat. When I stopped I lay there looking at the top of the plow sticking up over the hill. A little lump of snow broke loose and slid down beside me, then the plow backed up and disappeared.

I stood up and looked at the tracks as the first engine passed the end of the street. I scrunched down behind the ties so the engineer wouldn't see me, and I kept an eye on the hill in case the plow came back. The sound of the big diesels rumbled right through me.

The first engine went by, then another, and another and another, and a fifth, and then I got mad that Bucky wasn't there to see five engines. It seemed like his mom messed up more fun than any ten parents put together, including my mom and dad.

I pulled my mittens off and emptied my pockets. I picked out a couple good rocks, then moved around the pile of ties where I could watch the train cars coming at me out of the falling snow, but no one in the engines could look back and see me. Three old box cars went by, then a bunch of tankers, then a couple gondola cars loaded with scrap. After that came a bunch of box cars again, and they went on so long I stopped counting after twenty-three. There was a flatcar with something on it under a gray tarp, then some trailer cars loaded with containers, then all of a sudden a transport car appeared out of the snow.

I got a rock ready. The transport car passed and I threw the rock but it bounced off a fender. I got another rock real quick and threw again but I hooked it and missed everything. There was another transport car behind the first one and I got three more rocks off and hit a windshield with one, but it didn't break.

A couple more box cars came into view so I took a minute to pick out the heaviest rocks I had. When I had them in my hands I moved out from beside the ties 'cause I knew the engineer couldn't see me anymore. Two flatcars went by and then I saw more transports coming.

The first rock I threw hit the side window of a

green station wagon, but it bounced off. I wished I had Bucky's new slingshot 'cause it could break anything, but I didn't so I just threw harder. The next transport had the new panels on the sides so you couldn't hit the cars, but the one after that was open and I threw as hard as I could and missed everything again.

I went and got more rocks from my pile and threw them all as fast as I could, and I hit three different cars but no windshields. I looked at the rest of the rocks but they were all too small, so I dug in the snow but all I found was more weeds and I had to stop because my fingers were freezing.

I went out close to the ditch with the train going by only a couple feet away. I looked in the snow along the ditch, then I saw some rocks down through the ice that I busted over the air pocket. I kicked the ice out more, then kicked at the rocks and one broke loose that was as big as a softball. I looked up the tracks but it was snowing so hard I could only see as far as the next car.

I tried to practice throwing the big rock but it was heavy and my fingers were so cold it ripped out of my hand the first time. I picked it up again and backed up as more tank cars went by, then some hopper cars full of coal. They weren't as fun as the empty ones, which made a sound like a giant bell if you hit them.

I couldn't see the end of the train, but I could hear the couplers slacking and it sounded like there weren't many more cars. I backed up a little because I didn't want the man in the caboose to see me standin' there with a big rock, and right then a transport popped out of the snow.

I waited and picked out a shiny blue car on the second deck. When it came by I ran up and threw the rock as hard as I could, right at the side window. I knew it was going to smash the window to bits, but at the last second I saw the glass was already busted. The rock flew in the window and didn't make a sound.

The transport disappeared into the snow and I stood there, seeing the rock go in the window but not hearing the glass. I stood there even when the caboose went by and a man waved at me out the side window. By the time I remembered to run and hide the train was already lost in the snow. I listened to it, the wheels squeaking and pinging farther and farther away, and then it was gone.

I looked up the track toward the curve. I looked at the bare bushes and the trees draped in snow. I took a couple steps up the tracks to see if someone was hiding in the ditch, or at the bridge, but I couldn't see halfway there. I looked up the hill and the plow was gone and I couldn't hear anything. Not a car on the street, not a dog, not anything.

The snow kept falling and I stood there looking up the tracks for whoever busted the window. I thought it might be Pelican for a minute, or the Drury brothers, but I listened and no sound came down the tracks.

I looked toward the rail yard and I thought maybe it was a train that had gone by before, on another day, with the same transports and same cars, and maybe it was a window I'd already busted. But that didn't make sense so I went back to looking up the track with the snow falling harder and harder, until I couldn't see anything.

Everything around me was white and quiet and I got a sick feeling like maybe I was the only person anywhere. I looked at my hands and I couldn't feel my fingers. I walked over and picked up my mittens but I had a hard time pulling them on.

I kicked my toboggan to find the rope under the fresh snow, then I climbed the hill grabbing weeds with one numb hand and pulling the toboggan behind me with the other. When I got to the top I ran down the middle of the plowed street, and when I got home I stood the toboggan on the front porch and went inside.

It was warm and I could hear Mom and Dad and Megan in the kitchen. I took my coat off and listened to them laughing, then went up to my room and closed the door. I climbed on my bed and looked out the window, but it was snowing so hard I could barely see Mrs. Gale's house on the other side of our driveways.

Every time I thought about who busted the car window on the transport I saw myself standing up the line with a rock in my hand. I heard Megan squeal, and a few minutes later the furnace came on and muffin smells blew into my room from the vent.

The feeling in my hands came back prickly and burning. I tapped the window with a fingernail and watched the snow fall, and waited for Mom to find me.

BE MINE

~ February ~

When it was my turn I pulled my poster out from in front of my desk and went up beside Mrs. Blaske. She looked at her notes and said, "Our next instructor is going to teach us a little bit about the Russian alphabet." I stood the poster on a chair and looked at the class. They were all looking at me and the poster to see if I was gonna be interesting, or if they were gonna go back to being bored or worrying about giving their own speeches.

Bucky had his head down on his desk, looking at me sideways, but he'd already heard what I was doing my speech on so he didn't care anyway. Cindy Ree was looking at me like I was gonna do something stupid. The poster started to fall forward so I grabbed a corner and straightened it back up.

"The Russian alphabet has thirty-three letters," I said, holding the poster so hard I tore the edge. Mrs. Blaske grabbed the other side to help me. "Some of the letters are the same as ours, and sound the same, but there's others that are different. The first letter is an *a* like ours, but the last letter is a *ya*, which looks like a backwards *r*." I pointed to the poster where I'd drawn the letters in three rows, in upper and lower case. On my fingers I could still see pen marks from finishing the poster the night before.

"The third letter looks like a capital *b* but they say it like we say *v*. They don't have anything that looks like a *v*." I looked up and Cindy Ree was paying real close attention, and so were a lot of the other kids.

"Then how do they say *vodka*?" I looked over and Mike Craig was smiling like he was smart.

"I don't know," I said.

Mrs. Blaske said, "We'll wait until after the speech for questions, Mike."

I forgot what I was going to say next so I looked back at the poster. "The Russian alphabet has thirty-three letters," I said.

"You already said that," Cindy said, and I didn't have to look up to know it was her.

"I know," I said. "I'm going to read the alphabet and pronounce the letters."

"I think maybe we might learn a little more if we said them along with you," Mrs. Blaske said. "Listen closely, class."

I turned and looked at the class and all of a sudden they were paying attention like it was a film or something. Even Bucky sat up a little and put his arm under his chin. I looked at the poster and started reading.

I went pretty slow, and each time I said a letter the whole class said it back. Some of the letters were hard so I did them a couple times, and one I did three times. I could hear Cindy saying them louder than everybody else, and one time she said she didn't hear me right so I did that one again.

I got to the end and I wasn't nervous anymore and Mrs. Blaske had a big smile on her face. "Any questions now, class?" she asked. I looked around and Cindy and Mike Craig had their hands up. Mrs. Blaske called on Mike.

"How do they say *volleyball*," he said, a big smile on his face. Mrs. Blaske gave him a dirty look.

I took the poster and headed back to my desk but Cindy said, "Where'd you learn that?"

I looked at her and she was staring right at me, waiting for an answer. "I got the alphabet out of a book and made the poster from that. My mom helped with pronouncing it," I said. Cindy sat back a little, smiling.

Mrs. Blaske looked around and said, "Thank you. That was very interesting and very well done," then she smiled at me like she liked me. I went back to my desk and Mrs. Blaske said, "Cindy?"

Cindy got up with a book and some pieces of paper, but before she went up front she turned and said, "That was neat," right to me. I didn't know what to do so I kicked the poster in front of my desk. I looked over at Buck and he looked like he was asleep.

"My lesson is about origami," Cindy said. "Origami is the ancient Japanese art of paper folding." I opened my desk and pulled out a piece of yellow writing paper. "Many different animal figures can be made with origami, which involves not cutting or gluing the paper." I folded my piece of paper diagonally and tore off the extra, leaving a square.

Cindy showed a square piece of pink paper to the class, then made a few folds. "Only a variety of paper folds are used to create the shape desired." I made some folds on my square piece of paper. "Anyone can learn origami. All it takes is practice...and patience."

I looked up for a minute and I couldn't tell what Cindy was making, but she was concentrating on it real hard. She said, "This is an example of..." then stopped, because she messed something up and had to undo it. I made more folds on my paper and looked up again as she was finishing. "This is an example of an origami shrimp." Cindy held up her shrimp and it didn't look like anything except maybe a pink banana.

Cindy looked at Mrs. Blaske and said, "Can I do it again?"

"No, you did just fine." Cindy went back to her desk and sat down, still trying to fix her shrimp. Mrs. Blaske checked the clock and said, "Bucky?"

I looked over as Bucky sat up, rubbing his eyes. "Yeah?" he said, like he forgot he was in school.

"You'll go first tomorrow," Mrs. Blaske said, then the bell went off like she planned it that way.

"Okay," Bucky said.

"Don't forget your valentines tomorrow, class. And be sure to bundle up. It's twenty degrees outside."

While everyone got their stuff out of their desks and headed for the coat rack in the hall, I went over to Cindy's desk and put the origami duck I made on the corner by her origami book. She looked at it and said, "Where'd you learn that?"

"I don't remember," I said. "Maybe a book from the public library." Cindy picked up the duck and tried to see how I put it together. "You can have it if you want," I said.

"Thanks," she said, smiling at me. She took her book and my duck and went to get her coat, and I followed after her.

"Boy, that was boring," Bucky said behind me. "I almost fell asleep."

Cindy got her coat and her hat and went down the stairs. I watched her disappear, then I looked at Buck. "What?" I said.

"Nothing," Bucky said, putting on his coat and hat and grabbing his boots in his arms. "My mom's picking me up, so I guess I'll see you tomorrow."

"Okay," I said, watching him head down the steps. A moment later I heard one of his boots fall, then I heard him kick it down the next flight of stairs, and the next.

By the time I got my sweater on, and my coat and mittens and hat and boots, and got my hood up over my hat, I felt like I was the only person in the building except for the janitor. I went out the side door by the gym and the first couple breaths were so cold I wished I'd asked Bucky's mom for a ride home. I tried closing my mouth and breathing through my nose but that made my whole head hurt, so I jammed my chin down inside my coat collar and breathed in through my covered mouth and out through my nose.

It was cloudy again and the sidewalks were still covered with ice and frozen snow. I stuffed my hands in my pockets even with my mittens on and headed home, sliding on ice every chance I got.

Up the street two big crows were pecking at something by the curb. They flew away when I walked up and I could see they'd been eating a pink valentine cookie. The crows landed in a tree and watched me walk past. I didn't get how they made it through winter with only the same feathers they had for summer, but they didn't look like they cared about the cold at all.

I looked back when I got to Bowery Street and the crows were picking at the cookie again. I thought about my speech while I walked, and about Cindy Ree, and I felt good.

When I turned on my street I saw a woman way down the block. She was starting up Mrs. Wibbley's sidewalk from a car at the curb. I heard some kids yelling behind me and turned to look, but it wasn't anybody I knew. When I turned back the woman was gone.

I stopped and looked at the car again, then at Mrs. Wibbley's front door, then I saw something move and I could see the woman was lying flat on her back on the sidewalk. After a bit she put one arm up in the air, then it went down, then it came back up again.

I walked down to my house real slow, watching the woman roll over and get up on her hands and knees. She reached out and grabbed the strap of her purse, then stood up, her bare legs shaking below her dress. When she got to her feet and still had one hand on the ground she slipped again and fell straight back down on her knees.

I stopped by the big maple in our front yard and watched her get up again. Down at the dead end a car backed out of a driveway and headed toward me. The woman turned sideways and crawled off the sidewalk and stood up again in the snow. The car stopped and the driver watched her until she was standing all the way up. I could see one of her knees was bleeding.

The woman walked up to Mrs. Wibbley's house all bent over like she had the wind knocked out of her. Her purse was banging against her leg, and every few steps she froze like she just skidded on some ice.

It took a long time for her to climb the steps on Mrs. Wibbley's porch. She held the railing with both hands, and when she got to the top it seemed hard for her to push the doorbell. When Mrs. Wibbley opened the door and helped the woman inside the car in the street started going again. The driver and I looked at each other when he went past.

I got a shiver and remembered how cold it was. I ran up the sidewalk steps, skidded along the walk, then hopped up the porch steps like a rabbit.

*   *   *

After dinner Mom reminded me I had to finish my valentines, so I went up to my room and got all of the stuff and brought it back downstairs. I tried to take it in to watch TV with Dad and Megan, but Mom made me go in the dining room so I'd get it done. She did give me cookies and milk though, 'cause of how good I did on my speech.

I spread out the valentines and checked the class list and I only had ten done so far. Every kid in class had to get one this year, or you couldn't give any. It made a lot more work, but I thought it was a good idea 'cause it was pretty sad seeing Olin Johns only get two last year, and one was from the teacher.

I got the pen ready and looked at the next name

on the list. It was somebody I didn't like so I picked out one of the small valentines in the set that I got at the drugstore. By the time I got their name written and signed my name the cookies were gone.

I stuffed the valentine in its little envelope and wrote the person's name on the front and put it in the done pile. I looked at the empty cookie plate and listened for Mom, but when I went out to the kitchen she caught me before I could find the cookies.

I did two more valentines and crossed the names off the list. I put the valentines in their envelopes, then I had to take them out again to make sure which name went on the outside of which envelope. When I had the names on the envelopes I put the valentines back in, then I had to take them out again 'cause I was sure I put them in the wrong envelopes, but I didn't.

The phone rang and Mom answered it. "Oh my god," she said. I turned and looked in the living room. "You're kidding," Mom said. "Is she okay?" I heard Dad get off the couch, but she shook her head at him so he stood in the living room door and went back to watching TV.

"Sure," Mom said. "Okay. Okay. All right. Bye." Mom hung up and walked over to Dad. "Mrs. Wibbley's mother fell and broke three ribs."

"That's gonna hurt," Dad said.

"They're keeping her at Mercy tonight and Mrs. Wibbley is going to stay with her. She just wants us to feed her cat in the morning and make sure the house is warm enough for the pipes."

"Okay," Dad said, still watching TV.

"Is she gonna be okay?" I said.

"Yes, I think so," Mom said.

"What about her knees?" I said.

"I don't think she hurt her knees," Mom said, walking over and rubbing my hair. "It might be nice if you made Mrs. Wibbley a valentine too. She does an awful lot for you."

"Okay," I said. I picked out a pretty one and signed my name, and Mom helped me write *Mrs. Wibbley*. Dad went in and turned off the TV, then I heard Megan fuss a bit and he came back carrying her on his shoulder like a sack of potatoes. "It's gonna be colder tomorrow so I'll give you a ride to school," he said, then he took Megan upstairs to bed. Mom was back in the kitchen guarding the cookies, so I looked at the next name on the list. It was Cindy Ree.

I could still see her face looking at me when I was giving my speech. And her smile when I gave her the origami duck. I didn't remember seeing her like that before, all happy and smiling, but I had a perfect picture of her in my head like I'd taken it at school.

I stared off thinking about Cindy, and her blonde hair and her smile. I was thinking about her so hard I thought I heard her say, "That was neat!" again, but when I looked around it was only Mom walking by with laundry from the basement.

"What?" I said, like I was working hard and she was interrupting me.

"I didn't say anything," she said, taking the laundry upstairs.

I looked at the valentines, trying to pick one out for Cindy. I looked at the only big one in the set, which was the one I gave Buck every year, but I thought about giving it to Cindy. It had a little cupid in a towel, and he was shooting an arrow at a little boy. It had hearts all over it and it was pink and purple and orange, and the more I looked at it the more it seemed like something for a girl.

I looked through the valentines that were left and I couldn't find one that I thought would be just as good for Buck. Then I thought how he'd give me the big one from his set and get a little one from me and I didn't want that. And then I got worried that if I gave Cindy a big one and she gave me a small one I'd look stupid, and Buck or somebody else might notice and say something.

I wrote Bucky's name on the big one and put it by the pile and picked out a pretty red one for Cindy that was shaped like a big heart with an arrow through it. I signed it and put her name on it, then I put it in an envelope. I wrote her name on the outside as carefully as I could and put it on top of the pile with the others.

I did the rest real quick until I got to the bottom of the list, which was always Bucky Will. I put Bucky's valentine in the big envelope and signed it, but for a second I wished I'd given it to Cindy.

I ran up to my room and got the coffee can I'd decorated with construction-paper hearts, and the plastic lid that Dad helped me cut a slot in. Back at the table I put the valentines in the can through the slot, one at a time, until I only had Bucky's left. I had to take the lid off to put his in, but when I did I saw Cindy's envelope so I pulled it out and looked at it again.

I was still looking at it when Mom came back downstairs. "All done?" she said.

"Yeah," I said.

"Bed time then."

"Hey Mom?"

"What?" she said, coming over by me.

"Is this okay?" I showed her Cindy's name on the outside of the envelope. She looked at it real close.

"It's fine. I'm sure she'll be very happy to get it."

"Really?"

"Really. Now get upstairs and brush your teeth."

I stuffed Bucky's valentine in the can and put Cindy's on top, then I put the lid on again and went upstairs. While I was brushing my teeth I wondered if Cindy was brushing her teeth too.

*   *   *

The next day we had to sit through the rest of the speeches before we got our valentines. Bucky's was the best 'cause he had mouse traps with ping pong balls on them. He dropped one ball in the middle and it made all the mouse traps go off, and the ping pong balls went everywhere.

"All right, class, get your valentines out," Mrs. Blaske said. "Put your cans on your desk and make your deliveries."

I poured my valentines out on my desk and put the lid back on just in time for someone to shove in a valentine. I looked over and Cindy was on the other side of the room. I tried to pick up my valentines and go over there too, but I had too many to carry. I picked out the ones for the kids right by me and shoved them in their cans as fast as I could.

I took a few over to the next row, then I grabbed the rest and went around the back of the room to where Cindy was. When I got there she went up around the front and back to her desk, so I got rid of the valentines right by me but kept an eye on her. When I put one in Olin Johns' can he was standing by his desk, smiling. He hadn't delivered any of his yet and was just watching everybody stuff valentines in his can.

I had to take the top off to stuff Bucky's valentine in his can, and it was already pretty full. Bucky went by while I was putting his lid back on. "Happy Valentine's Day," I said.

"I just put yours in," Buck said. "You got a lot."

I looked over at my can and Cindy was putting the lid back on. I froze right where I was and Mike Craig almost ran over me. I couldn't take my eyes off my can, because if Cindy Ree had to take the lid off it meant she gave me a big valentine. I looked down at my hands and the little envelope with her name on it.

I stuffed a couple more valentines into slots and went over by Cindy's can, but she got there at the same time and I didn't want her to see me giving her the little valentine. I got rid of a couple more and went back to her desk again, but right when I thought she wasn't looking she turned around and smiled at me. "Happy Valentine's Day," she said.

I looked down at the two Valentines in my hand then back at her. "Happy Valentines Day," I said. I took Cindy's in one hand and looked at the other. On the envelope it said *Mrs. Wibbley*. I looked back at Cindy and she was standing right by her desk, looking right at me.

I looked out in the hall and said, "Is that your coat that fell down?" Cindy turned and took a couple steps toward the door. I smashed her valentine in the slot. It wouldn't go in at first 'cause the can was stuffed, but I mashed it in before she came back.

"No, it's not mine."

"Oh," I said, then I went back to my seat with Mrs. Wibbley's valentine. I tossed it in my desk and pulled my can under my chin and looked at all the valentines inside.

Olin came by and handed me his valentine and said, "Happy Valentine's Day."

"Thanks," I said, taking it from him and looking past him at Cindy, who was looking in her can too.

"Is everybody done but Olin?" Mrs. Blaske said. She looked around the room, then at the clock. "All right, you may look at your valentines."

There was one big sound as everybody poured their valentines out on their desks, then all you could hear was envelopes being ripped. There were two big valentines in my can, and I could tell the first was from Buck so I grabbed the other one. I ripped it open and it said *Happy Valentines Day – Cindy*.

I stared at the card, then I laid it down on my desk and stared at it some more. I looked over at Cindy and she was talking with some girls at her desk, showing them the valentines she got. I wished I could take the one I gave her back.

Bucky came over, holding the big valentine I gave him. "Hey, yours is just like the one I gave you." I opened Bucky's card and it was.

I showed him Cindy's valentine. "Cindy gave me a

big one," I said.

"Yeah, me too," Bucky said. I looked up at him. "I think she gave everybody a big one." I looked at the valentines on a desk beside me and there were two big cards in the pile. "They must have cost a lot," he said. I looked around and some kids had three big valentines in their piles.

I put Cindy's valentine down and opened another one in my pile. Olin came up and showed me the valentine I'd given him and said thanks. He went away and then Bucky went away, and I kept opening the rest of my valentines until I was done.

*　　*　　*

At the end of the day Mrs. Blaske gave me a note that said Dad couldn't pick me up like he planned. It had been too cold to have recess, but looking out the windows I could see the sun was shining and the wind wasn't bad. When I had all my stuff on I picked up my valentine can and decided to go out the front door instead of the side. When I did I almost ran into Cindy Ree coming back in.

"Hi," she said, stopping close to me, her face peeking out of her hood.

"Hi," I said.

"Happy Valentine's Day."

I could see her eyes up close, how blue they were. "Where'd you get all those big valentines?" I said.

"My mom got a bunch from a friend of hers," she said. "She owns a card shop and they didn't sell very well. I wanted to pick my own but I had to use those."

"Oh," I said.

"I liked the one you gave me a lot," she said. "It was really neat." Then she ran up the stairs and disappeared.

I waited a long time for her to come back down but she didn't, so I went outside. Even as cold as it was, the sun was warm on my face. I thought about Cindy while I walked, and when I got home I was surprised I was already there.

THE BURGLARY

~ *March* ~

It had been a pretty good week, what with school being out for Easter and the weather finally letting up. I found the most eggs during the neighborhood hunt, and that was the day the clouds broke up and the sun got a chance to melt the old snow away. Mostly there was just black dirt and dead plants everywhere, but in the shadows there were still piles of dirty snow that made it look ten times worse, like nothing would ever grow again.

Megan didn't find anything but a bag of peanuts at the hunt, and she cried about it till I told her I didn't find anything my first time either. I told her I remembered hearing somebody yell, "Go!", but by the time I found a place to look all the other kids were counting what they'd found. I gave her a green and orange egg and she smiled and went to show Mom and Dad. I didn't tell her I cried too.

I'd been playing a lot with Terry and Jed Figgin, who lived down the block a few houses up from the tracks. We'd been goin' to each other's houses and riding bikes a lot, but not sleeping over or anything like that. They had some okay stuff to play with, and we didn't get in a lot of fights, except for me and Jed. He's a grade younger than me and Terry, and always wants to wrestle whenever we tell him he's stupid, and he always looses.

It had been warm enough that the ground dried out some from all the melted snow, so we were riding our bikes up and down the hill by the tracks. The hill's real steep in some places, but there are piles of matted old weeds to wreck in if you crash on the way down, or don't make it all the way up to the top.

Jed always tried to show off so we wouldn't think he was chicken, and right about the time Terry and I were getting hungry he decided to ride over the pile of railroad ties that had been sitting there for months. He got up one side okay, but then his back wheel spun on some oil the sun had brought out and he flipped over sideways. When he got up he was holding his mouth and trying not to cry. We could see blood running out between his fingers and when he finally let me look I got kinda sick. He'd cut his lip pretty good and I thought he was gonna need stitches.

"You'd better get home," I said.

"It doesn't hurt."

Terry yelled at him like he always does. "Then what're you cryin' for?"

"I'm not cryin'!" Jed yelled back, spitting blood.

"I'm going," I said. "I'm hungry."

"We got some peanut butter 'n' jelly," Terry said. "You got enough?"

"I think so," he said, then pointed at Jed. "He sure ain't gonna have any."

"I am too!" Jed yelled.

We beat Jed back to his house 'cause he had to drag his bike off the ties and try to keep from bleeding all over himself. He ran in while Mrs. Figgin was getting the sandwich stuff out, yelling, "I get some, I get some," and dripping blood on the kitchen floor.

Mrs. Figgin let out the same sound my mom does whenever I get hurt, like she was trying to suck in all the air in the room. "Jed!" she yelled, blowing it all back out. "My God, what have you done!"

"It ain't nothin'," he said, trying to suck in his lip and catch more of the blood.

Mrs. Figgin tried looking at it but he wouldn't let her, so Terry started making his own sandwich like he knew it wasn't gonna get done if he didn't. Mrs. Figgin finally pulled Jed's hand away and took a good look at his lip, and when she did she made that sound again.

I looked over and Jed's lip looked a lot worse 'cause it was swelling up. "Are you okay?" Mrs. Figgin said, running her hand over his head and through his hair.

Jed said, "It don't hurt," but the way she was touching him was making it tough for him not to cry. He looked at me watchin' him and turned away. I saw Terry was done so I started making a sandwich. Mrs. Figgin took Jed into the bathroom down the hall.

Terry looked after them. "Pretty good wreck," he said, his mouth full of peanut butter.

"He's probably gonna have to have stitches," I said. "You ever had any?"

"Yeah, on my big toe. Stepped on some busted glass and cut right through."

"Did that on my heel once," I said, "but I didn't

have any stitches." I jammed my fat peanut butter and jelly sandwich into my mouth.

"Ever?" he said.

I tried to talk but I couldn't get my mouth clear enough to say anything so I shook my head. Terry took another bite of his sandwich and we both stared off at nothing 'cause we could hear Jed crying.

Mrs. Figgin came back and put some ice cubes in a bloody towel and told us to clean up after ourselves. She said she was taking Jed to the hospital to see if he needed stitches.

Terry said, "When's Dad coming home?"

Mrs. Figgin said, "I don't know, Terry. I wish you'd stop asking me that."

"Well when is he?"

"Terry, I don't know! Why don't you watch out for Jed a little more and quit worrying about your father!"

Terry scratched his arm like he does when he's worried, then took another bite of his sandwich. Mrs. Figgin said she was sorry and went back to take care of Jed. She seemed tired and mad, but at least she didn't blame me for what happened. Bucky's mom was always blaming me for everything, even if it was Bucky's idea in the first place.

Terry said he was going upstairs for a minute, but what he really did was go half up the stairs to a window and watch them drive away. I didn't want to go in the living room and catch him so I stayed in the kitchen and finished my sandwich.

The door to the back porch was open so I went out and looked at their backyard. Everything was matted down and tired-looking and I wished it wasn't. I wanted to see green plants and yellow dandelions, but there wasn't any color anywhere. Even their red slide was all rusted brown.

The sun went behind a cloud and it felt cold again right away. With all the shadows gone their backyard looked like winter again and I hated it. When I looked out a side window of the porch I could see clouds all over the sky to the north.

I decided right then to go home, but when I turned to go I saw a partly rolled-up poster lying on a little table with some other junk. It was like one I had at home, where you color it in yourself.

I unrolled it more and I could see all the different butterfly shapes and I knew it was the same one I had. "Hey, Terry!" I yelled.

I looked for the colored marking pens and they were on the table too, same as mine. I unrolled the rest of the poster and I could see Terry'd been working on the same big butterfly as me. It was pretty good, and the more I looked at it the more it seemed like the way I'd done mine.

Terry called from the kitchen. "Where are you?"

I was looking at all the colors in the butterfly and how they seemed like the ones I'd used. I could see the pen marks in the reds and purples, where the pens had gotten dry. I could see where the green pen had gotten mushy and ripped the paper. And I could see the blue mark where I'd gone outside the edge of the butterfly into a leaf.

Terry was standing in the door to the kitchen, looking at something under the table. I looked down at a shelf holding a glow-in-the-dark yo-yo like mine, and a picture book of animals I had, and a forty-eighth scale model of a P-51 Mustang that I put together and painted blue with red peace signs on the wings. On the floor under the shelf was my rubber boa constrictor and my fielder's glove.

I stared at the stuff a long time. I stared at it and I knew I couldn't be staring at it 'cause it was all back in my room. The Mustang wasn't mine somehow, even though I was looking right at it and I spent more time putting it together and painting it than I ever had on anything. I picked it up and saw somebody'd busted off one of the propeller blades. I saw where the glue had run when I glued the body together, and where the blue paint hadn't been dry all the way and mixed with the red. I put the plane back and picked up my glove. My ball fell out on the floor. "This is my stuff," I said.

"No it ain't," Terry said, scratching at his elbow. "Who says?"

"I say!" I yelled, and I wanted to hit him and cry at the same time. "That's my poster and my pens and my plane, and my yo-yo and my snake and book and ball and this is my glove!" I shoved the glove at him, showing him where I'd written my name on the heel.

"That ain't your name," he said.

I hadn't bothered to look 'cause I'd been so sure, but when I did I remembered Terry and Jed couldn't read real well. I turned the glove over so he could read the name right-side up.

"Well you didn't write it real well," he said. "It looks Chinese."

"Where'd you get this?" I said, and even then I didn't really think they took it right out of my room.

"Jed found it. Out back in the alley. That's what he said."

"My stuff was just sitting in the alley and he just found it?"

"That's what he said!"

"Well what would it be doin' sittin' out in the stupid alley!"

"How do I know!" Terry was getting red in the face. "It's your stuff, you're the one oughta know!"

"Well I didn't put it there!" I kept looking at my stuff like it wasn't really there, and I could see Terry looking at it like he wished it wasn't, but it was. I wanted out of there and I wanted my stuff home, and I wanted Terry to tell me he took it and he was sorry. I wanted it never to have happened, and I wanted it to be summer again.

"I'm goin'," I said, picking everything up, but it was hard to hold it all.

"How do I know that's all yours, anyway?" Terry said. "Could be some of Jed's stuff in there."

"It's all mine," I said, going past him through the house. I could hear him following me but he didn't try to stop me. When I got outside I saw my bike leaning against their front porch but I went past it and down the sidewalk.

Terry was standing on the porch, yelling at me. "I'm telling Jed when he gets back! If any of that's his you're gonna get it!" I didn't look back or listen to him. "You can't leave your stupid bike here either!"

I got as far as Mrs. Wibbley's then the Mustang fell on the sidewalk and busted off another propeller blade. I got so mad I jumped on it and smashed it to pieces, and dropped some of the other stuff. Right away I wished I hadn't crushed it but I picked up the other stuff and kicked the big pieces of the plane into the street. I didn't stop again until I slammed my bedroom door shut behind me and set everything on the floor.

I was gonna put it all back where it went, but all of a sudden I thought about other things that might be missing. I'd think of something then I'd have to find it, but I couldn't even feel good about it 'cause I'd think of something else and have to find that too. The more I looked for things the more I found things I forgot I had, and that got me thinking maybe something was missing that I couldn't even remember to look for.

I got so mad I just sat down and looked at the stuff on the floor, and mostly I couldn't remember the last time I'd played with any of it. I picked up the yo-yo and got up and tried it but it ran right off the end of the string. I remembered busting it the last time I used it, but I couldn't remember when that was. It seemed like a long time since I'd seen the snake, too, and when I looked at it close I could see where the rubber was cracked and the tail was getting ready to fall off.

I heard someone come in the house, then up the stairs, then Mom opened the door and asked me what my bike was doing down the block in the middle of the street. I told her I didn't know. She told me to go get it and to take a coat 'cause it was getting cold out. On the way out she said I better straighten up my room.

I hadn't been inside long but it was a lot colder out like she said. The clouds had come back and they were like a gray blanket across the whole sky. You couldn't see where the sun was anymore, even though it was still light out.

I walked down the street, balancing on the curb. I could see my bike down the block, lying in front of a parked car. I was glad to be out of my room until I came to the pieces of my busted plane. I thought about trying to glue it back together, but when I looked around I couldn't find one of the wheels.

I picked up the pieces I could find, thinking I could use them for spare parts on something else, but by the time I got down to my bike I was sick of looking at what I'd done. I walked across the street and threw the parts into the storm drain.

My bike was okay as far as I could tell. It looked like there might be a few new scratches, but I couldn't tell for sure because there were so many old ones. I rode back home real slow, coasting in and out of driveways along the way. I closed my eyes a lot, feeling the cold on my face and not wanting to look at the clouds. I thought about having Dad help me paint my bike like he said he would. I thought about painting it green like a maple leaf, but when I looked at our maple tree in the front yard all I could see were buds on the ends of the branches.

I rode up the driveway and around back to the garage. I knew the folding doors were rusty and the garage leaned a little so you couldn't ever get them to close all the way, but after I hid my bike behind a stack of screens I tried to close them anyway. First I tried pulling the doors together, then I went inside and pushed each one out flat from behind, but the harder I pushed the more they bounced back the same. I pushed and let up and pushed and let up, and each time they bounced out almost flat and sprang back as if I hadn't touched them. I got so mad I finally kicked one door and then pushed it as hard as I could, but all I managed to do was pinch my hand so bad it made me feel like crying again.

I waited until the pain went away and I didn't cry and I promised myself I wouldn't ever. Looking up at the top of the doors I could see where one was partly off its rollers. I tried to get it back on, but when I lifted the bottom of the door the rest of it came off and the whole thing hung there like a busted wing.

I wanted to pull it down the rest of the way. I wanted to bust out the windows in the garage and kick in the screens, but I kept seeing my smashed plane in the storm drain and hearing each piece hit bottom.

It took a long time but I finally got the door back the way it had been. I was cold when I went inside, and I bugged Mom too much about dinner so she got mad and sent me to clean up my room the way she does when I know she means it.

I put most of the stuff in my toy box, but I kept the yo-yo out to see if I could fix it. Megan came in and bugged me for some of my stuff so I let her have what she wanted after I scared her good with the snake.

I got some string off one of the rolled-up kites in my closet and made a slip-knot on one end. I put the loop over one side of the yo-yo and pulled it tight, then I let the yo-yo hang and ran the twist out of the string. After a couple swings the yo-yo climbed right up, but then I got bored playing with it pretty fast.

I put the yo-yo under my table lamp so it would

soak up light, but a while later I put it in a desk drawer beside a science kit I got for my birthday. When I went down for dinner I closed my door.

*   *   *

The next week at school wasn't real good and I was glad when it was Friday. I'd told Bucky what happened and pretty soon everybody knew about it. I had math and gym with Terry, and by the end of the week he was trying to get me about every time he saw me. He even got in a fight with Marty Helger 'cause Marty called him a thief.

That's what Bucky told me anyway, when he came over Friday night. He wanted to see the stuff they took so I got it out and showed him, and he got the same creepy feeling I had. I didn't tell him what I'd done to the Mustang.

"Maybe we ought to steal something of theirs," Bucky said.

"I already thought about it," I said. "They don't have anything worth takin', and besides they're probably waiting for me to try something like that."

"Yeah. And you don't want anyone calling you a thief."

"Yeah," I said, and I laughed 'cause Marty Helger is almost twice as big as either of us. I looked at all the stuff I'd found at the Figgins' and it was like I just brought it back again. "I've only been by their house a couple times since," I said, "but I thought I saw Jed looking at me out an upstairs window."

Bucky really got the creeps then, so we decided to

sneak down the alley and spy on their house as soon as it got dark. We went down to watch TV, but Dad was watching something on the news about a big storm. I made Bucky go in the kitchen and ask Mom if we had any cookies. I knew we didn't but Mom'll make them for anybody if they ask, as long as it isn't me. Bucky came back and said Mom was gonna make cookies if she had time before her class, and that wasn't till eight so I thought we had a good chance of getting some.

When it was dark we went down to get our coats, but we didn't do it fast enough and Mom asked Dad what the temperature was. Dad said it was twenty-seven degrees and Mom said it was too cold to be out at night, like I knew she would. When I said it wasn't we got in an argument and she threatened me with not making any cookies.

We went to watch TV again but Dad was watching another news show. He got mad at me for saying it was the same thing about the same stupid storm, but it was. We went up to my room but that was boring so we went down the hall to my sister's room and made her give back the toys I let her have.

Since we couldn't go out we decided to sneak around the house, spying on people. We took a peak at Mom but it didn't look like she was making cookies. We started to sneak up behind Dad to scare him, but we decided that was a bad idea and kept going along the hall into the study. Bucky pulled the door shut real quiet by hanging his weight on the knob, then we crawled under the desk, staying out of the light the streetlight threw on the floor through the open blinds.

We left the light off in the study 'cause you could

see it under the door when it was on. We heard Mom ask Dad where we were, and when he said he didn't know she said she wasn't surprised. We laughed real quiet and listened to Mom yelling for us upstairs.

"Think we can sneak back upstairs?" Buck said.

"Sure. We'll have to watch out for Mom, but Dad's gonna be watchin' TV."

"What about your sister? She'll tell."

"She's in bed. Mom's worried she's getting a cold."

There was something safe about being in the dark and not having anyone know we were there. It made me feel better than I had since I found my stuff at Terry's. "It'd be fun to sneak into Terry's house like this, wouldn't it? Maybe take something just so they'd know we'd been there."

"Don't they have a dog?" Bucky said, sounding like he does when he thinks he might get hurt.

"It got hit by a car last year."

"Oh," he said, and I could tell he was remembering his own dog that got killed a long time ago. He grabbed me. "Let's make like we're trapped behind enemy lines, trying to get out. We got secret plans and if we get caught they'll torture us."

"That's dumb," I said.

"What's dumb about it?"

"It's just dumb. Who's gonna know we got secret plans if they catch us?"

"Well, what if we take something?"

That was a better idea, and right away I knew what we'd take. "Come on," I said, and Bucky followed me around the corner of the desk to some shelves set in the wall. We were careful to crawl under the light coming in from the window again, but it hit part of the shelves and I had to put my arm in it when I reached up and pulled down a little wooden box.

"Remember this?" I said, moving it into the light so Bucky could see it.

"Yeah, you got those silver dollars in there," he said, feeling the carvings on the sides and the top. "I forget how it works."

I showed him where the piece of wood slid back on the side, then I pressed the hidden catch and a little drawer popped out one end of the box. I pulled the drawer open and looked inside but the shadow from the streetlight made it all black.

I shook it a little and held it over my hand, then Bucky said, "What's the matter?" I could hear the wind hitting the storm windows and I couldn't remember hearing it like that before. I stuck my fingers in the drawer and I felt sick, like crying again, only worse.

The silver dollars came from my mom's father, and she'd given them to me as long as I didn't play with them. There were three of them, and the oldest was from eighteen ninety-six. They were all real heavy and it felt good just holding them.

Bucky said, "Maybe your dad moved 'em," but I remembered showing Terry the box. I hadn't even cared about showing him the silver dollars then. Just the box and the secret way it opened. I closed the little drawer and held on to the box, feeling the cold wind coming through the cracks in the windows.

When we went out in the living room Mom yelled at us for hiding from her. I kept squinting my eyes in the bright light. When I asked Dad if he had the silver dollars he said no.

Mom looked at me hard and said, "Why?"

It took a long time, but Bucky helped me tell all of it. I kept having to wipe my eyes to see, but him being there made it easier not to bawl out loud. Except when Mom first got that the silver dollars were gone. She looked sad and got mad and blamed me, then she cried a little and hugged me and we stayed like that.

When she finally went to class Dad looked to see if anything else was gone, and that's when it hit me maybe they'd come back after the first time and taken more of my stuff. Bucky helped me check my room 'cause he knows most of what I got, but we didn't find anything gone.

We stayed awake a long time that night. We heard Mom get home, and her and Dad talking, but then the house got quiet. Bucky kept coming up with ways Terry and Jed could get killed in a car wreck or run over by a train, or have their house burn down, but mostly I listened to the wind and thought about summer and climbing trees. By the time we fell asleep I had two blankets on my bed and I was still cold.

In the morning, when Dad called Mrs. Figgin, it was even colder, like winter again. When he got off the phone he said she didn't know anything about the coins and that her boys said I was lying. I got mad again, but Dad asked if I showed the box to anybody else. I said I didn't know but I had. I hated it when Dad said we couldn't prove they'd taken the coins. I reminded him about the other stuff I found at their house but he said it was my word against theirs, and maybe if I'd told him about it right away things would be different.

When Mom and I took Bucky home she visited with Buck's mom awhile and told her about the silver dollars. I begged her not to but she went ahead anyway. While they were talking in the kitchen Buck and I sat in the living room and thought up a million ways to get back at Terry and Jed, but Bucky's mom heard us and Mom made me promise to stay away from them forever.

When we got home a man in a truck was driving away from our house and Dad was sweeping sawdust out of the hallway and off the front porch. His breath was blowing out his nose and mouth, and he waved at us as we pulled in the drive.

He showed me the big gold locks the man had put in the front and back doors. They were shiny, and when you turned a knob on the inside a big bolt came out the side of the door and stuck in a new hole in the wall. Dad showed me a key and said it was mine, and he and Mom told me how important it was not to lose it.

They kept talking to me and I kept opening and closing the door, turning the knob and feeling the bolt and how strong it was. Dad said they'd have to have the locks changed if I lost the key. Mom said it was sad we had to have them put in at all.

I turned the knob real slow, again and again, so I could see right when the bolt went into the wall. When they finally made me stop I locked the door and pulled on it as hard as I could. And I never lost the key.

THE ELM

~ *April* ~

It was the first warm spring weekend, and Mom and Dad and me and Megan were visiting the Dawson's farm just north of Summit. It had rained a lot early in the month, but then the sun came out day after day until the ground dried out. A week later everything that had been brown was bright green, from the grass to the bushes to the new leaves opening up on all of the trees.

Mom and Dad met the Dawsons when I was born. Mrs. Dawson and Mom shared a hospital room when she was having me and Mrs. Dawson was having her daughter, Kelly. We'd been going to their farm to visit as long as I could remember, and I liked it 'cause they had woods and fields you could run around in without any grownups telling you what not to do.

As soon as we got there Kelly and me filled our canteens, stuffed our jacket pockets full of Girl Scout cookies, and headed down the hay road. Kelly's in the Girl Scouts but she lives on a farm so it's okay. She's not like girls like Cindy Ree, who have a ton of badges but couldn't climb a tree to save their life.

We took Kelly's dog Bronco with us, but he ran off

down the hay road and was out of sight by the time we got to the trees. He's a giant scary-looking dog, like a cross between a German shepherd and a horse, but he never bites. I like having him around 'cause he runs off the foxes and coons, which can be mean and might have rabies.

We stopped where the hay road entered the woods and I pushed some dry brush back, looking for a patch of raspberries. I found the hard purple vines with the big spikes on them, but there weren't any berries.

"It's too early," Kelly said. "They won't be out until summer."

"That's too bad," I said, then I looked through the tangle of vines at the base of a pine tree behind them. "Is that a morel?" I said, pointing.

Kelly came over, looked and said, "Yeah, a big one. My dad's been out three times and hasn't found any."

"Let's get it for him," I said, trying to push through the raspberry vines and getting stuck good. I looked for an easier way to get to the tree but I couldn't see any.

"Let's get it on the way back," Kelly said. "That way we won't have to carry it."

"Okay," I said, taking a drink from my canteen and opening a package of cookies.

When we got going again we took our time, looking at all the new plants coming up in the woods. Kelly knew a lot of the plants by name, but I spotted a few I knew too.

As we walked the hay road twisted back and forth, leading us from one field to the next, but we'd been down it so many times I knew every rut. The only animal we heard turned out to be Bronco, who ran out of the woods on one side of the road and into the woods on the other like he was chasing something we couldn't see.

"You ever camp out here, Kelly?"

"A couple of times with my mom and our Girl Scout troop. It was boring. One of the girls cried."

"Figures," I said, finishing the package of cookies. I stuffed the wrapper in my pocket and thought about eating the rest but decided not to.

The sun was high but there weren't many leaves on the trees so it stayed warm on us the whole time. Looking at a big bare tree I pointed and said, "That's a maple, ain't it?"

"No, oak," Kelly said. She picked up an old brown leaf with rounded edges and showed it to me. "This is an oak leaf. Oak trees drop acorns. Most maple leaves are spiked and the trees drop those little propellers." Kelly pointed at a few on the ground behind me, and I could see the tree they came from.

"I know," I said. "We got a big maple in our front yard, remember?"

"Oh yeah," Kelly said, 'cause she'd been to our house plenty of times.

I picked up a couple of the little green propellers, tossed them into the air, and they spun away like helicopters. "I think the elm in our backyard is sick," I said. "They cut down two more on Summit Street." I took a drink from my canteen and Kelly took a drink from hers. "I wish they'd do something about it."

"It's Dutch elm disease," Kelly said. She pointed. "Dad says it's got them over there and there's nothing anybody can do."

I looked at two big old elms and I couldn't see any buds or new leaves on the ends of the branches. I hated seeing them like that and was glad when the hay road turned up a long hill. On the way to the top Kelly saw a blue jay and I saw two cardinals. Kelly said it was the same bird twice, but I told her anybody could tell the difference.

At the top of the hill the hay road opened on to an old clover field that hadn't been cut the year before. Clumps of dead clover were heaped on the ground, and every once in a while a red-winged blackbird would fly up out of a clump, cawing and screeching and hanging over our heads until we went away.

"Let's go down to the back pasture," I said.

"We're supposed to stay out of the creek," Kelly said. "It's way up with all the rain lately. Bronco!"

I looked where she was yelling. On the far side of the field Bronco was running in crazy circles, chasing something we couldn't see. Over his head two red-winged blackbirds whirled around like a little tornado. Bronco stopped still for a moment, then ran straight for the trees with the blackbirds on his tail.

"Bronco! Come here!" Kelly ran after him but he disappeared. "Bronco!"

"Forget it," I said. "We'll never find him."

"I don't want him killing," she said.

"I thought you said he doesn't catch anything."

Kelly walked back. "He doesn't," she said. "But a couple weeks ago he came home with blood on him. We don't know where it came from."

"Oh," I said, looking down in the clover for anything that might be there. "Has he had his shots?"

"Yeah." Kelly called for Bronco again, then gave up and we headed for a big walnut tree at the far edge of the clover field.

I ate the rest of my cookies and kept an eye on the trees as we crossed the field. I tried not to imagine what Bronco's bloody face would look like if he caught whatever he was chasing.

The hay road started up again by the walnut tree and headed down the side of a steep hill. We followed it as it curved through vines and brush growing in from both sides.

"Hey, look," I said. "Deer droppings."

Kelly looked at the pile of little brown pellets, then pointed at tracks leading into the trees. "They went through there. We've seen a lot of them this year."

"Let's follow 'em," I said.

"We'd never get close," Kelly said. "They'd hear us and run off before we ever saw 'em. It's better to stay on the hay road. We won't make as much noise and we can see farther."

I thought about following them myself, but then I remembered Bronco and I didn't want to run into him alone. "You're right," I said, picking burrs off my pants.

When we got to the bottom of the hill the hay road ended in two old tractor ruts leading into the back pasture. The pasture was surrounded with trees, and full of dry corn plants that hadn't been harvested. A lot of the plants were only shoulder high, but in some places they were over our heads.

As we walked down two rows next to each other I said, "Why didn't somebody pick this corn?" The rows got taller and taller until all I could see was the tops of the trees around the field.

"It stayed wet too long. The farmer who rented the field said he wouldn't get enough yield."

"Oh," I said, looking at a hole in the ground. "You ever see any corn snakes?"

"I don't think so. Mostly just garter snakes, and they don't hurt anything." Kelly looked at the hole too. It felt scary in the corn, and I was glad when she yelled, "Last one to the trees is a corn snake!"

She got a good head start from cheating, and I tripped on a broken corn plant almost right away, but I caught her before the trees and won easy. "You scared the deer off with all that yellin'," I said, pretending not to be glad to get out of the corn.

"Who cares," Kelly said. "I've seen plenty."

I could tell she was mad about losing the race, so I picked more bristles and burrs off my clothes and didn't say anything else. Kelly scratched her head, then brought her other hand up and felt around. "See if this is a tick," she said, leaning her head toward me.

I turned her toward the sun coming through the trees at the edge of the field. I parted her hair where her hands were, but I couldn't see the tick because she kept feeling around for it. "Get your hands out of the way," I said.

"I don't want it to get in," she said, moving her hands back a bit.

I looked around and didn't see a tick, but she had her hair pulled so tight I couldn't see anything unless it wandered right out in the part.

"Let go," I said.

"Hurry up," she said, kinda angry.

"You're not helping," I said, knocking her hands away. I felt around until I felt a little bump in her hair. I pulled the hair apart and slapped her hands away again. "I almost got it," I said.

Pushing the last few hairs away I saw the tick wandering around on top of her head like it was lost in a forest. When I tried to pick it out I pulled Kelly's hair and she jerked away.

"Ow," she said, reaching her hands up again.

"Hold still – I almost had him!"

"Is it in? Don't pull it out if it's in!"

I found the tick again, but he was hard to get hold of. After a couple tries I got him between my fingers but I had a couple of her hairs, too. I thought about trying to get him again but Kelly was squirming around too much so I just pulled the tick out, hairs and all.

"Ow!" she yelled. "You pulled it out! I told you not to pull it out!"

"I didn't! Look!" I held up my fingers and showed her the hairs. "It was just a couple hairs."

She held out one hand and rubbed her head with the other, feeling for the tick like she didn't believe I got it. I dropped the hairs and the tick in her hand and she looked at the tick real close.

"Don't thank me or anything," I said.

"Thanks," she said, watching the tick walk around on her hand. I watched her looking at it and decided I liked her a lot. There's not a lot of girls who'll play with a tick, or not cry when you pull their hair.

"Sorry about your hair," I said.

She threw the tick in the bushes. "That's okay," she said, pulling a thorny vine back and heading into the woods. "It didn't hurt."

From the pasture to the creek wasn't very far, but it always took a while because everything grew so thick down there. We kept getting stuck on wild rose bushes and nettles, and I could tell Kelly was still mad about the tick or maybe the race because she didn't care how bad she ripped her clothes on the snags.

We found a deer trail and the going got easier, and a few minutes later we were standing on the bank of the creek, looking at how full it was compared to usual. "It's gonna be hard finding a place to cross," I said. "All the trees we used before'll be under water."

I looked at the mud-colored water. It didn't seem to be moving too fast, but you couldn't see what was under the surface at all. I knew I could swim it, but I didn't want to get caught on a branch or pulled under by a whirlpool.

A little farther on we had to climb a big mound of branches that had been piled up where the creek made a sharp turn. Along the way Kelly found a snake skin and I found what I thought was a coon skull, but Kelly said it looked like a cat.

As we followed the creek the trees got bigger and thicker and the branches locked overhead. We found a vine as big as a rope that we climbed a ways, but we didn't climb too high in case it pulled loose.

We ran along the edge of the creek until we could see where it was going next, then cut through the trees to catch it when it turned back, all the time looking for a place to cross. A couple times I looked around and it seemed like we were on the other side of where we'd just been, but I knew we hadn't crossed the creek so we kept going.

We found what we thought was a beaver dam and almost fell in trying to see if it would hold our weight. We tried crossing in another place but it wouldn't hold us either. Then, when I was sure we would never get across, Kelly spotted exactly what we were looking for.

A dead tree had fallen across the creek, its roots up in the air like muddy spikes on our side, the trunk and busted limbs smashed into the mud on the opposite bank. It was so wide it was like a bridge, and so thick that half of it was under water. Where it blocked the creek there was a log jam packed with branches that had floated downstream, and some of them stuck up so you could grab them almost like a railing.

Kelly reached up over her head, pulling some dirt off one of the dead tree's rotten roots, and most of the root came with it. "I remember this tree," she said. "Creek must'a brought it down a couple days ago."

"Then we'll be the first ones across," I said, climbing up through the back of the roots and walking out on the trunk. From the middle the creek looked a lot wider, and I could see the water was moving faster than I thought. It slipped under the trunk dead quiet, and I got a little sick thinking about being sucked under the tree, or pinned against it by the force of the water.

Kelly climbed up behind me and I looked over at the other bank. There were a few trees on that side, but past the trees was a sunny clearing full of weeds that looked like they were eight feet tall. I saw a spot where I thought deer had been through pretty regular, and right then I thought I heard some rustling.

"You hear that?" I said, turning and whispering to Kelly.

Kelly listened a minute. "It's the water," she said.

I listened, and it did sound like the creek running through the branches jammed up against the trunk, but it wasn't. Then I heard it again and I knew it was coming from the clearing. "It's in those tall weeds," I whispered, so quiet I almost couldn't hear myself.

We watched the weeds and some of them twitched a bit. There was a pause, then the weeds swayed for a moment in another place before falling still. Another patch quivered, then another.

Kelly whispered in my ear. "It's a deer." When she said it the weeds stopped moving, then whatever it was came right for us. I turned to run off the log but Kelly was in the way, holding her stupid finger up to keep me quiet.

I turned back and almost jumped out of my skin when Bronco stepped out of the weeds and onto the bank. He was holding his upper lip off his teeth and the fur on his face was red. His teeth looked as big as a bear's.

"Bronco, what did you do?" Kelly yelled from behind me. "You better not'a killed anything, Bronco!"

As Bronco climbed up on the other end of the trunk I grabbed hold of a branch to keep from falling off. "Stop calling him!" I yelled, not taking my eyes off him.

Bronco walked slowly toward us, his lip twitching. I could see his tongue, and grit in his teeth. Drool fell out of his mouth onto the tree trunk. "He's got rabies!" I screamed.

I pushed Kelly back and she fell against the roots. I tried to help her up but my foot slipped into the creek on the downstream side and I fell against her. I woulda slid right in if I hadn't grabbed her canteen belt.

"Get out of here, Bronco," she yelled. I tried to pull my leg out of the creek, but right then Kelly got up and her canteen belt pulled free, and instead I slid in up to my thighs.

Kelly broke off a branch and threw it at Bronco but he kept coming. He made a funny, high-pitched whimpering sound as his face came close to mine. I took one look in his watery, bloodshot eyes and turned my head 'cause I knew I was finished.

"Bronco!" she screamed. "You killed a skunk!"

And then I smelled him. He reeked like he caught a blast right in the face. It was so strong I couldn't breathe. I closed my eyes and grabbed for a branch in front of me. I pulled on it as hard as I could to get me out of that creek and away from that horrible smell but the branch came off in my hand.

For a second I thought I'd fallen in because of all the splashing, but when I opened my eyes I was still hanging on the side of the tree and Bronco was splashing around in the creek with me holding on to his leg.

"Aah – I got rabies!" I yelled. I let go of Bronco and he paddled toward me but I kicked water at him and he turned away. I felt Kelly grab my collar and pull as Bronco paddled to the middle of the trunk, but the water was moving too fast and he floated downstream.

"Come on," Kelly yelled, helping me up onto the tree trunk. She pulled me back the way we'd come but I could see Bronco trying to get out on our side.

"This way!" I yelled, pulling her the other way. I ran across the trunk to the far side without even thinking about it, and Kelly came right behind me.

"What a stink!" she said, plugging her nose. "I can't breathe!"

"We gotta get away from him," I said, real quiet. I pushed into the tall weeds and we headed straight for the sun, ignoring the foxtails whipping our faces and the crisscrossing deer trails. The smell seemed to stay with us forever and I was sure I could hear Bronco behind us the whole time.

When we stepped out of the weeds we were at a stand of trees I didn't remember seeing before. We turned back and watched the weeds but we didn't see them moving, so we sat down on a big old mossy log and drank some water.

It was still and quiet under the trees, but that only meant I could hear every little sound around us. When my breathing got quiet I could hear even more, but no matter which way I tilted my head I didn't hear anything that sounded like a dog. Then, right when I was listening as hard as I ever listened in my life, and wondering whether it was quiet because maybe her dog drowned in the creek, Kelly yelled, "Bronco, I hate you!" right in my ear, as loud as I ever heard her yell.

"Shhhh!" I whispered, ducking down. "He'll follow us." Kelly got quiet but she was still mad. "Besides," I said, leaning close but keeping my eyes on the weeds, "I don't think he got that skunk. I think that was dirt on his face from trying to wipe the smell off on the ground."

Kelly smiled a little at that. "I hope the skunk did

get away," she said. "Serves that dumb dog right."

"You think he can get out of the creek okay?"

"Yeah, he's a good swimmer. Maybe it'll take some of the stink off him."

I smiled. "Think how bad a skunk must smell to a dog. They smell ten times better than we do! P.U.!"

Kelly smiled again and shared her last package of cookies with me. After we ate I emptied the creek water out of my shoes and wrung out my socks.

I was putting my shoes back on when I thought I heard Bronco behind us. I turned around and it was a squirrel climbing down the biggest tree I ever saw.

I nudged Kelly and pointed at the tree. "Wow," she said, tipping her head back to follow the trunk into the sky.

We walked over to the tree, looking up at the main branches and the bright new leaves popping out way up at the top. It was only then that I noticed the whole clearing we were in was under that one big tree.

"That's the biggest tree I've ever seen," Kelly said.

"Me too," I said, thinking it was twice as tall as the trees in my yard, which were bigger than any of the trees in my neighborhood.

I tied my squishy shoes while Kelly walked around the tree. It was so big I couldn't hear her when she was on the other side. When I looked up again I could see a big rip in the bark, way up where the main branches split off from the trunk. It looked like lightning had taken off a branch.

I turned around and looked at the tree we'd been sitting on. When Kelly came back around I said, "That tree we were sitting on used to be a branch, right up there."

"Wow," she said, looking at the branch lying on the ground, then back up where it came from. "It's as big as a tree itself."

Kelly took my hand and said, "Let's see how big it is around." We pressed against the tree and stretched out as far as we could, but we could still lean back and see each other. The only part of Kelly I couldn't see was her other arm.

"This is the biggest tree in the world," I said. "Nobody's gonna believe me when I tell 'em we found it."

"There's bigger ones in California," Kelly said. "I read about 'em in school. But I'll bet there isn't a bigger one in Summit. There can't be."

Looking up I couldn't tell what kind of leaves the tree had 'cause they were so far away, but lying on the ground I found a few old elm leaves that hadn't rotted during winter. "I bet this is the biggest elm tree in the world. Even in California."

"Maybe it is," she said.

I tried to see how many steps it took to walk all the way around, but I kept looking up and forgetting where I started. The bark was rough and hard and I could grab hold of the edges and climb pretty easy, but even going up a little way was scary 'cause it was more like climbing a wall than a tree. I didn't like not being able to get my legs around it, or the way the tree leaned out over my head no matter where I tried to climb.

When I jumped down we laid on our backs and stared up at the branches reaching into the sunny sky. We watched a couple squirrels chase each other around and around in the treetop, jumping on branches so small I was sure they would break. A couple times they were right over us, flying around, and I creeped Kelly out by telling her one of them might fall on her face.

We looked at the tree a long time and I never got bored. I tried thinking of things I'd rather be doing, but there weren't any. "I could stay here forever," I said.

"Me too," Kelly said. I looked at her and she looked happy, like she had forgotten about Bronco. I looked back up and I could see the top of the tree twisting real slow in a breeze I couldn't feel.

I didn't want to go, but the sun was peeking in under the branches on one side of the tree. On the way back we found an easy way into the raspberry vines to pick the morel for Kelly's dad. "You think it'll get sick too?" I said to Kelly. "That big elm?"

"I don't know," she said.

"It's too big to get sick," I said, and I thought about the elm in our backyard. It was big too, going all the way from the house to the alley, but it was turning brown in parts. A man was coming to see if it needed to be cut down.

Walking back to Kelly's house we drank the rest of the water in our canteens. "I think it's gonna keep growing," I said. "Get bigger still."

"We can come back and see," Kelly said, but I decided I wouldn't ever go back. I didn't want to see its leaves turning brown, or see a red *x* on its trunk.

When we got to the house we got a lecture about how late we were and how worried everyone was. We tried to get out of it by showing them the morel, and telling them about Bronco and the skunk, but everything I said just made Dad mad. He said we'd scared our moms for no good reason, that we weren't being responsible and we should have known better. Then he made us apologize and said we better mean it.

I heard myself saying, "I'm sorry," like I meant it, even though I didn't, and right then I knew I would go back to see that big elm the first chance I got. I'd go back 'cause it might live a hundred more years and always be there, spread out so big the rain would never fall on you if you were under it.

I looked at all the trees around me, and I heard some birds fighting off in the woods. Mom looked at me funny and reached down and felt my wet pants, and I knew she knew we'd been to the creek. I think we would have been in a lot more trouble if Bronco hadn't shown up right then.